Black-Hearted Bitch

A Kell Digby Crime Novel

Lynn Kear

ALSO BY LYNN KEAR

Relative Innocence

Tighter, Tighter

Murder in a Buckhead Garden

Laurette Taylor: American Stage Legend

Evelyn Brent: The Life and Times of Hollywood's Lady Crook

The Complete Kay Francis Career Record: All Film, Stage, Radio and Television Appearances

Kay Francis: A Passionate Life and Career

FIRST EDITION

THIS IS A WORK OF FICTION. NAMES, CHARACTERS, PLACES, AND INCIDENTS ARE THE PRODUCT OF THE AUTHOR'S IMAGINATION OR ARE USED FICTITIOUSLY. ANY RESEMBLANCE TO ACTUAL PERSONS, LIVING OR DEAD, BUSINESS ESTABLISHMENTS, EVENTS, OR LOCALES IS ENTIRELY COINCIDENTAL.

Printed in the United States of America

COVER DESIGNER: KV HERNDON

Copyright © 2013 Lynn Kear
All rights reserved.
ISBN: 0615855539
ISBN-13: 978-0615855530
Grey Fedora Books

For Kimber

ACKNOWLEDGMENTS

Drue Barrett whipped Microsoft Word into shape while being patient, cheerful, and instructive. Thank you, my friend.

Amy Dawson Robertson generously agreed to read a draft of this novel before publication. As always, her comments were much appreciated.

Kimber Herndon read many drafts and spent lots of time with me talking about the characters, plot, and settings. Her editing was spot-on, and her enthusiasm for the project propelled me through some dark times.

PART I

1

"Got a job if you're interested."

I was drinking a cup of coffee on the balcony of my Chicago high-rise. It was March and fucking freezing. I liked how the hot coffee felt in my mouth. I held the phone in one hand and wrapped my other hand around the mug. I liked how that felt too.

"Come for dinner tonight," Rosa said. "It's complicated. I'll grill some steaks."

I didn't say that I wanted the job, but I'd take it, complicated or not. I was bored out of my fucking mind and getting squirrelly.

When people ask what I do, I say I'm a security consultant. I have unusual hours and travel a lot, so I had to come up with something vague yet plausible.

"You mean, you look at people's homes and businesses and then come up with a plan on how they can be safer?"

"Something like that."

Only it's nothing like that. I'm not actually a security consultant, even if that's what it says on my tax form. Rosa fills them out for me. I guess she's my employer. She owns Ironclad Security Consulting LLC and supplies bodyguards or killers, depending on what people want. I don't do much guarding, though I have in the past. That's how I started before I became Rosa's best hit man. I've been doing it for almost six years. I've done it so long I've been thinking about doing something different. I'm just not sure what.

My typical day starts with a cup of coffee and then a workout at the condo gym. For two hours, I run and lift weights. Then I shower, eat lunch, and go to the shooting range where I practice for an hour. In the afternoon, I swim in the condo's indoor pool. If I have an assignment, I do prep work or kill someone. If I don't, I go back to my condo.

I usually eat out for dinner, often alone. In the evening, I watch TV, usually switching back and forth between HGTV and ESPN.

I check my portfolio at the brokerage firm at least once a week, run calculations, and try to figure out how much more money I need before I can quit. It's hard to know when you have enough.

I'm usually in bed before ten. I occasionally date, but I'm never going to be the world's best partner. I'm not good about doing the things that you have to do to keep the other person happy, like returning phone calls and making plans for the future. I'm not even a good friend. I know people, and we go to Cubs games or see movies, but I don't hang on the phone with anyone. People say that I'm self-contained. I think they mean that I don't need anyone.

Rosa lives in Glencoe, one of those North Shore suburbs with old brick and stone mansions and lots of old, thick trees. We used to live together until I bought my Lake Shore Drive condo a few years ago. She helped me pick it out and furnish it. We didn't break up because we were never together. We occasionally sleep together, and when we do it's good. I've known her longer than anyone. Sometimes I think we'll end up together when we're old.

"Hi, Wonder Girl," Rosa greeted me when I arrived at her

door.

"Smells good in here," I said, stamping my boots in the dark foyer. It hadn't snowed in a few days, but there was gray sludge everywhere. By March, everyone is sick to death of snow and winter.

"I've been cooking for you, sweetie," she said. She handed me a cold Amber Bock.

I saw a chocolate cake under a glass dome. Baked potatoes were wrapped in foil on the countertop. A hand-turned wood bowl held mixed greens with black olives and tomatoes. The dining room table was set with fine china, a white tablecloth, and candles. Rosa is a class act.

"Filet mignon okay?" she asked.

"Sounds great." I sat on a sleek black leather barstool at the breakfast bar while she pulled two steaks out of her refrigerator. She grilled them on the fancy stovetop and gave me the particulars.

"It's a husband," Rosa said. "Outside of Atlanta. You'll get one hundred."

"What's complicated?"

"The wife—the client—doesn't live with him. So his schedule is—" Rosa waved her hand, studying the sizzling steaks. "He walks just about every morning at Stone Mountain Park. Between nine and eleven. You learn the park, the layout, his schedule, bam. It needs to be done soon. You'd have to leave tomorrow. You need to be there a few days. Maybe longer. I hear it's lovely this time of year. It's easy in Georgia. Not enough GBI staff. Big backlog at the crime lab. Piece of cake, that's what it is." It'd gone from 'complicated' to 'piece of cake.'

"Tomorrow," I said.

"I'll get you a rental. I've got your credit card, phone, and ID ready."

These days I don't ask why someone wants someone else dead. I did at the beginning, but it was always the same two reasons. Money and love. Someone has it, and someone else wants it. Like Rosa says, "It's always the money, honey. Unless it's the love."

Rosa was quieter than usual while we ate. I figured she was tired. Business was good, both the legal and the illegal side. Rosa has always done things by the book. She's a CPA and has a degree from the University of Chicago. She never attempts to defraud the IRS. All taxes are reported and paid quarterly. It's important, Rosa explained, to look like a legitimate business.

"Well," she said before we ate the cake, "do you want the job?"

"How long a drive is it?" I didn't care. Like I said, I'd already decided.

"Thirteen hours. For you, twelve."

She pointed to a manila folder on the table. I looked through it. It contained several color and black-and-white photographs of the client's husband. Hank Kingsley was around forty, balding, with a circle beard. A notation said he was 5'9 and weighed 150 pounds. He wasn't much taller than me. He looked fit, but it wasn't going to do him any good.

In the folder was a pamphlet on Stone Mountain Park. On the front, in big letters, it said, "Rediscover your sense of Adventure." I'd think about it.

"This is where he hikes?" I asked, looking through the brochure.

"Yep. Just about every morning. Same time. Same trails. There's a map in there. It's a large space, but you'll see it's do-able. Want some coffee?"

I nodded. Rosa ground the Colombian beans and started brewing half a pot. I picked up our plates from the dining room table and carried them into the kitchen.

"Just set them on the counter," Rosa said.

I did as she requested and felt her behind me. She turned me around and kissed me. She unbuttoned one button, then a couple more. It surprised me. It had been months since we'd slept together. It might have been around Thanksgiving. She had my shirt off, tossing it to the floor. She unbuttoned my jeans and slid her hand between my legs. That sealed the deal. We went upstairs to her bedroom and had some fun.

"Happy St. Lisa's Day," Rosa said an hour later. According to Rosa, St. Lisa was the patron saint of lesbians. Whenever we had great sex, we'd say it was St. Lisa's Day.

"Merry St. Lisa's Day."

"Coffee's ready, sweetie," she said, pulling me up to a seating position.

"Are you still seeing the realtor?" I asked as we ate cake and drank coffee in her living room.

"I haven't heard from her in a few weeks. She was more interested in the house than me," she said and laughed.

I laughed too.

"You haven't seen that cop again, have you?" she asked.

"No." I gave her a 'get real' look. This was a sore subject. I'd had a one-nighter a few months back with an Elmhurst cop who I'd picked up in a dyke bar. Rosa blew a gasket when she found out.

"Good. You seeing anyone?"

"No. Thanks for cooking for me. It's nice. Great cake." I was genuinely touched. It was baked-from-scratch. I had a large piece and then another half.

"Take a couple pieces with you tomorrow. I don't need a whole fucking cake sitting around here."

When I got ready to leave, Rosa embraced me again, gently biting my neck and my shoulder. "I love you," she said close to my ear.

I kissed her. "I love you too. You worried about me?"

"I always worry about you, sweetie."

"I'll be fine." I made a face. "Is there something different about this one?"

"No," she reassured me. "I just want you to know that I love you. Maybe we should think about living together again when you get back."

It was an odd statement, but I pretty much forgot about it after I left. I had to pack, so I could leave early in the morning.

Shortly after I got back to my condo, Rosa called. "Don't forget the cake," she said.

"I've already packed it." I had. I'd put it in my backpack, already loaded with toiletries, makeup, candy bars, nuts, gum, guns and ammo, and water bottles.

"Call me when you get there, Kell," she said. "Take care of yourself, sweetie."

"Always."

"Have a good time—but not too good."

2

Kids today don't know the thrill of driving a car for the sheer pleasure of it. Gas is too damn expensive, and it's a fucking shame.

I love to drive. Rosa had rented me a top-of-the-line Lexus that practically drove itself. I picked up the car in the early morning darkness when it was ten degrees in Chicago. It wasn't long before the car and my buns were toasty.

I smiled when I saw the ID and credit card. Lisa Bruce. Rosa liked to use that name. We came up with it one day when we were trying to figure out the gayest name in the world.

Soon I was in Indiana. I hadn't made any stops. Yeah, I like driving, but I also like arriving at my destination. I finally had to fill the tank. I peed and got a Dr. Pepper from the machine. It was too messy to eat the cake, but that's what I wanted. Instead, I ate salted peanuts. Rosa tries to get me to eat healthier. I've gotten better, but I still eat like a kid. I make hamburgers in the morning and eggs at night. Sometimes I'll have pop and a piece of cake for breakfast. I don't feel like a grownup yet. Maybe I'll eat better when I do.

There was a sameness to the road. This was all interstate. Everything looked identical, no matter if you were in Illinois, Indiana, or now Kentucky.

The light was muted. It was winter in the Midwest, and the

sun was hidden. The roads were dry, but there were snow drifts on the roadside. The depressing slush followed me all the way to Tennessee.

I've lived in Illinois all my life. I was born and raised in Woodbury, a pretty little town on the St. James River. The funny thing about Rosa is that she was my babysitter when I was a kid. No, she wasn't a pervy babysitter who seduced me or anything like that. She was a nice Jewish girl who lived a few blocks away with her parents and brother on a riverfront home. Her dad was a surgeon at St. James-Woodbury Hospital, and her mom was a dietician. Rosa started babysitting me, an only child, when I was six. She's eight years older, so she was a teenager.

Rosa was a cool babysitter. She didn't just put me in front of a TV and tell me to shut my yap. She took me to museums and movies. We walked on the riverbank, and she acted like she was interested in my ramblings. She read my poetry and critiqued it without any bullshit. She took me serious. My parents knew they could depend on Rosa. They even hired her to work in the Digby Art Gallery on State Street where they specialized in folk and ethnic art and did pretty well.

Rosa eventually went away to school. We reconnected when my parents died in a car accident while on a buying trip in Kentucky. I was sixteen and got sent to live with my mother's sister and her husband in Grand Ridge, a tiny Illinois town in the middle of nowhere. Aunt Mary Beth and Uncle Jim were religious nuts, I was a hellion, and it was the worst time of my life. I played Jim Carroll's "People Who Died" day and night, waiting for someone to tell me to knock it off. They never did.

Out of the blue, when I was close to graduating from high school, Rosa showed up. She took me for a drive, looked at me, and asked, "Want to go back to Chicago with me?" She worked out something with my aunt and uncle, and after graduation I moved into her house.

It was at least a year or so later before we started sleeping together. I seduced her, and she felt guilty for a long time. "Kell," she said to me, "you can always say no." I didn't want to say no.

She made me quit smoking when I moved in. "You're a pretty girl, but you'll ruin your looks if you don't stop." I had nervous energy after I quit, so she enrolled me in a bunch of fitness and martial arts courses. She also paid for me to take, get this, criminology courses at Chicago Circle. We vaguely talked about me possibly joining the FBI or Secret Service. It's hard to remember what we were thinking, but it's hilarious now. She still sometimes says, "You'd be good at it. Think about it."

She'd already started Ironclad when I moved in. She knew some tough guys, and it was a real bodyguard outfit when she started. She occasionally hired me. To be honest, it was mostly babysitting, but the pay was great. Anyway, before I knew it, I was working more, so I dropped the whole school thing.

I don't know how or why it occurred to her to try me out as a killer. I guess she just looked at me one day and thought 'Hmm.' She sat me down and asked me how I'd feel about it. "Do you think you could kill someone?" I think that's how she posed the question. The pay was a lot better than being a bodyguard. We tossed the idea back and forth before she sent me on my first job.

It was a local job, a slimy politician named Randy something who'd rubbed someone the wrong way. I shot the guy on Michigan Avenue. It wasn't supposed to be done there, but I panicked—hey, it was my first time—and nailed him not far from the Art Institute. I wasn't smooth, professional, or good, but I got the job done. My second hit went according to plan. I killed a rich husband in Evanston for a cheerful lady who called me "honey." The dude was old and went for walks on his tree-lined street. I drove by one evening and blew him away. I think Rosa wondered about me after the first hit. After the second, she gave me a funny look, and said, "You appear to have an aptitude for this."

For my third hit, I traveled out of state. Rosa sent me to Los Angeles to kill a short, fat, hairy film producer. That one went weird. The guy's female business partner ordered the hit. She also requested that I tell him why I was killing him. Trust me, it's easier to shoot someone in the back than in the face with their eyes looking at you. Rosa, of course, made her pay extra for this. The crazy bitch also wanted me to pretend to be a prostitute. It was a pretty complicated setup, but somehow it was fixed so that when he ordered a girl he got me. I'd gotten all dolled up and looked like a high-class trollop. I certainly didn't want to fuck or fuck around, so shortly after I arrived at his rented mansion, I pulled out the gun, aimed, and said, "This is for being a lying, cheating bastard." The expression on the guy's face was a mixture of humor, horror, rage, and, strangely, pleasure. "Black-hearted bitch," he said in a monotone just before I fired. I always wondered if he meant me, his business partner, or someone else.

"He didn't know you well enough to call you that," Rosa later said. If you think about it, what she said takes on different meanings.

Anyway, I always figured he knew who'd paid to off him. I'd like to think that I'd know if someone went to the trouble to have me killed.

In those days, I couldn't let the kill alone. I'd follow news reports until it wasn't reported anymore. I don't do that now. I'm not curious about what happens afterward. I mean, who the fuck cares?

My Lexus was gliding. I wanted real food. I stopped to fill up and ate at a truck stop just outside of Monteagle. It was country-themed with red gingham tablecloths and waitresses in matching dresses. The waitresses weren't particularly good-looking, but the hostess wasn't bad. She had on a wedding ring and looked about twenty. I couldn't imagine her life, but she didn't seem to mind. In fact, I got the feeling that she thought she was better than everyone else because she was a hostess, not a waitress.

I ordered a cheeseburger basket because it came with French fries and coleslaw. I was hungry. It wasn't bad, especially with lots of catsup. It made the next long stretch more tolerable.

I got to Atlanta around five in the evening. Rosa had been right about how long it'd take. She'd also given me a heads-up about the time change. It was five o'clock Chicago time. Six in Atlanta. I adjusted my watch and the car clock.

It was still daylight in Atlanta. It'd be getting dark in Chicago. I'd left ten degrees and overcast skies and arrived to sixty degrees and sunshine. Life was good. I pulled up to the hotel on Peachtree, parked the car in underground parking, and stepped outside onto the street. I felt dazed after driving so long, but once I hit the sunlight I was energized. The heat was a baking warmth. I could get used to it.

The hotel was fine. I knew it would be. Rosa wouldn't put me in a fleabag, but this one was extra special. Once I got to my room, I showered and changed my clothes. I was hungry again and knew what I wanted.

"Is there a place around here that serves eggs all day?" I asked a buff black guy at the front desk.

"Waffle House is just down the street, ma'am." He pointed. "There's an IHOP a couple blocks that way," He pointed the other way.

"Which one's closer?" I asked. I couldn't bear to get back in the car.

"Waffle House," he said. "You can get there in five minutes on foot."

I thanked him and went on my way. I made it in less than five minutes, walked in, and sat at the counter because the few booths were full. The oversized plastic menu was loaded with pictures of breakfast items. I ordered a cheese omelet with toast, bacon, and hash browns with cheese and onions. I could have ordered grits instead of hash browns, but I've never had them in my life, and didn't feel like making a major life change. I ordered a Coke too. I was, after all, in Atlanta.

I watched the cook prepare the food. He was fast and worked the grill with ease. The food was better than I expected. Hot and fresh. Of course, I wasn't expecting a lot.

"Princess of Power, I've been worried about you," Rosa said when I finally phoned her after getting back to my room.

"I got in around five your time. I got something to eat before I called." I was flat on my back on the bed. "Have you ever eaten grits?"

"I don't think so. What are they?"

"I'm not sure." I wasn't sure if I had the vocabulary to explain them.

"Something's come up, sweetie," Rosa said, quickly changing the subject.

I groaned and rubbed my forehead. I had a dull headache. I usually get one when I travel. Rosa tells me it's because I don't drink enough water. I don't drink a lot of water because I don't want to pee seven times on a twelve hour trip. We go round and round on this.

"It's the client," Rosa said. "She wants to meet you."

I closed my eyes. I didn't want to go back out. "You think it's a good idea?"

"You need to reassure her. She's freaking out. Can you meet her tonight? I'm afraid she's gonna bail."

I sighed. "Will she come here or will I have to drive?"

"You shouldn't meet her at your hotel. She suggested a time and place."

I was too tired to think. I'd let Rosa do that. "It's your call."

"Lenox Mall," Rosa said. "In the food court near the Chinese restaurant. The mall isn't far from where you are. Just

14

drive about a mile north, and it'll be on your right. 8:30."

I didn't have much time. I put on a charcoal pantsuit with a white blouse, tied my hair back, and put on black pumps. No way I'm putting on makeup, I said to myself. Since I refused to do the makeup, I hastily put on a pearl necklace and earrings. I hustled out of the room so I wouldn't be late.

3

I had to haul ass through Lenox Mall because I fucked up and parked on the wrong side. It was 8:29 when I stood at the top of the escalator and looked down on the food court. I spied a lone woman sitting at a white plastic table in front of Wok Yourself. Her back was to me, and she was fiddling with her phone.

I rode the escalator down, and when I got a few feet away, the woman turned to face me. My first thought was, damn, I should have worn makeup. She was flat-out gorgeous. I mean, wow. Tall, long dark hair and eyes, sensual mouth. Her jaw was square, and she had a dimpled chin. She must have been a model or actress before she married. Maybe a high-end working girl.

She was dressed cute too. A black lace dress and matching shoes. Several thousand dollars' worth of jewelry. Diamond earrings and an enormous rock on the ring finger of her right hand.

"Mrs. Kingsley?" I asked.

"Yes," she said, motioning me to sit. "Thank you for coming. I wasn't expecting a woman. I guess it makes sense. I just don't know. This is not my thing at all."

I remained quiet. I was supposed to reassure her, but instead I was checking her out. She was fine. Her voice was one of those smoky, jazzy things. This was going to be okay.

"I don't see how it can work," she whispered. I could barely hear her. I leaned in. She lowered her voice even more and moved closer to me. "Without me being a suspect."

I caught a whiff of her perfume. Chanel No. 5. The old Chanel No. 5—not the new formula. I wanted to touch her hand, squeeze it, tell her I'd kill her no-good husband and go to prison and die for it if she wanted me to. I still hadn't said anything because I was off in fantasyland.

"You'll have an alibi," I finally said. "There'll be nothing to tie it to you."

We were so close our faces were almost touching. I didn't care if we were acting suspiciously.

"People will always think it was me," she said.

Truer words were never spoken. I was almost giddy from fatigue as well as being hot for Mrs. Kingsley. "Let's get naked," I wanted to say.

She misunderstood my silence.

"I know you do this kind of thing all the time, but I don't," she said.

"Not all the time."

She smiled. I got the feeling she liked me.

"Your boss said you have a one hundred percent success rate."

"In everything."

"You're confident. I like that. It's just that I can be a bit intuitive."

What the fuck did that mean? I leaned back.

"I get feelings, you know," she said. "Sometimes I think he knows. He couldn't possibly, but I'm worried. How quickly do you think—"

"Soon."

She nodded. "Would it be wrong to see you again?"

Hell, yes, but that was fucking tough. "It might be helpful,"

I said. "Give me information that will speed things up." I was talking bullshit. I got the idea that she wanted to hook up. I'd be out of my fucking mind to turn it down.

"I'd like that." Her fingertips briefly touched mine.

I took out a small spiral-bound notebook, tore out a page, and hastily wrote down 'Lisa Bruce' and then my phone number next to it. It was for the burner phone. It'd work until I threw it away after the kill. Rosa and I used cheap cell phones that did or didn't do something. I didn't understand it, but Rosa did.

I handed Mrs. Kingsley the piece of paper. She stared at it for several moments, then tore it into little pieces, stood, walked to a nearby trash can, and dropped the bits of paper into it. She returned to the table. "I have an excellent memory," she said with a smile. "The mall's closing soon. I need to go."

"Where'd you park? I'll walk you to your car."

"I'm just outside," she said, pointing to her right. "I'll be okay, but thanks for asking."

It was probably a good idea because I would have had a hard time keeping my hands off her.

On the way back to the hotel, when I should have been going over the murder plan in my head, I was thinking about all the different ways I could do Mrs. Kingsley. It wouldn't have gone like this when I first started. I was totally by the book. No deviation from the plan. I was like a robot and never would have strayed from routine. But after doing it so many years, without anything terrible happening, I'd gotten looser, more careless. Success has a way of doing that.

"How'd it go, sweetie?" Rosa asked, when I called after getting back to my room.

"Did you ever do a face-to-face with her?" Rosa hadn't made any comments about Mrs. Kingsley's looks.

"Everything on the phone. Why?"

"Just curious. It went okay. I think I calmed her down. She might want to talk to me again. I told her we couldn't make it a regular thing."

There was a long silence on Rosa's end. "It's in your hands," she said. "You'll know what to do."

Yeah, I knew what to do. After I hung up, I turned on ESPN and ate a piece of chocolate cake with my hands. It tasted so fucking good that I ate the second piece too.

The next morning I walked down to the Waffle House and ate an egg and cheese biscuit before I drove to Stone Mountain Park. I took Peachtree Road to North Druid Hills down to Highway 78. It was a straight shot from there. It took maybe thirty minutes from my hotel. Not a bad ride at all.

I saw the top of the granite mountain a few miles outside the park. It's not something that you're expecting. Tufts of green were at the top, but it was essentially a huge fucking gray rock. Pretty impressive and not like anything we had in Illinois.

I took the exit to the park and drove up to the entrance. Lines of cars were waiting to get in, but they moved quickly. There were four gates. Each was attached to a tiny granite building that held one attendant. The digital sign said the entrance cost was ten dollars per day or thirty-five for an annual pass. I planned on coming daily for several days, so I sprang for the pass. The elderly woman employed to collect the money took my cash and then spent what seemed like hours putting the bills in her drawer. I got irritated, turned my head, mouthed, 'Hurry the fuck up,' squeezed the steering wheel as hard as I could, and took a deep breath.

The old lady finally handed me the sticker and a brochure. After leaving the gatehouse, I pulled off to the side of the road so I could read through the brochure. I was supposed to adhere the sticker to the inside windshield. Since the car was a rental, I'd have to use double-sided tape. According to the pamphlet, the park officials didn't want me to do that. Probably afraid people would trade the pass back and forth. Tough. That wasn't the only park rule I was going to break.

I got back on the road, parked in one of the main lots, and studied the map. There were several trails as well as a five-mile sidewalk that looped around the base of the mountain.

The "carving" was the main attraction—a towering bas relief sculpture that featured Civil War dudes on horses. The park—get this—was a Confederate War memorial. Streets were named after Stonewall Jackson and Robert E. Lee. It was like one of those alternative historical novels where the Confederacy won the fucking war. I grew up in the Land of Lincoln, so this amused me.

I continued scrutinizing the map. I planned to return the next day and walk the loop, paying particular attention to trail entrances and parking lots. I stayed at the park for about an hour. I would have stayed longer, but I got a phone call.

"Lisa, this is Mrs. Kingsley."

"Good morning."

"I was thinking we should meet again. Is that okay?"

She sounded nervous. I found it adorable. Getting together was fine with me. I'd been hoping she'd call.

"What part of town are you staying in?" she asked.

"I'm on Peachtree, not far from where we met last night. Not a good idea to meet at my hotel. Your car can't be seen there. Is there somewhere—"

"There's a Kroger close by. Can we meet there?"

A grocery store was a good idea. "The one by the post office?" I asked. I'd seen it on the way to the park.

"Yes."

"What time?"

"When can you get there?" she asked.

Mrs. Kingsley was eager to see me. I tingled. "Half an hour."

"Great," she said, sounding relieved. "I'll meet you in the produce section."

"From there I could drive you back to the hotel. So we can talk." I cringed, wondering if I'd gone too far.

"Sounds like a good idea."

I drove fast and arrived in less than a half hour. Mrs. Kingsley was standing by the apple display in Kroger's produce section.

We smiled at each other.

"I'll pick up a six pack of beer," I said.

She gave me a funny look. I figured I might have crossed a line. Maybe I blushed. It's not easy to make me blush.

"It's Sunday," she said.

I had no idea what she was talking about. "You can't buy beer on Sunday in Georgia," she said.

"*Why?*"

She thought for a minute. "I don't know. I never thought about it."

What kind of fucked up place was this where you can't buy beer on a Sunday? Where they name roads after Civil War generals who got their asses kicked?

"My place isn't far from here," she said. "I'll get some beer and come back. I don't mind. Really. I live just a couple blocks away."

We couldn't risk being seen at her house or apartment or wherever she lived. I waved my hand. "It's okay. I thought it'd be nice to have."

"I wouldn't mind a beer," she said. "You can order a drink at a restaurant or bar on Sundays, but we probably shouldn't do that."

"All right. I'll wait here. Anything else I can't have on Sundays in Georgia."

She smiled. "Not that I can think of."

She went on a beer run while I strolled up and down the aisles picking up a few things. It was mainly to kill time, but I tossed bananas, apples, a couple bars of dark chocolate, hot chips, and a six pack of Dr. Pepper in the basket. She found me in the snack aisle. "Want anything?" I asked.

"No, thanks. I've got the beer in the car."

We transferred the beer from her car to mine and drove to the hotel. Rosa would never have approved. It was unlikely I'd ever be connected to the murder, but if I was, it was possible there'd be a hotel video image of us together. It was a chance worth taking.

Once we got to my room, Mrs. Kingsley put the beer in the mini-fridge. She was more relaxed than she'd been the previous night. I must have done a good job reassuring her.

However, when we sat down, a shadow passed over her face. "I have to ask you something," she said. "This may sound weird."

I had no idea where she was going with this. I nodded.

She stared at me for a moment. "Who's Kelly?"

I'm sure my face flushed. "I don't know," I said.

She frowned. "I keep getting the name Kelly or something like it in my head. Maybe Keller. I told you last night I'm intuitive. I keep hearing it. Last night when I met you, it kept popping into my head."

My real name is Kelleher Digby. Kelleher was my mother's maiden name. Nobody ever calls me Kelly, but it's awful close to Kell, which everyone calls me. How could she know that? Still, I couldn't tell her my real name. Rosa would have a fit.

"What else are you getting?" I asked.

She didn't want to tell me. It messed with me. Maybe she *was* psychic. Maybe it was a warning of some kind. For her or me. "Tell me," I urged.

She shook her head. "That's the strongest. I had no idea that you were going to be a woman. When I met you last night—" She started to say something but stopped. "I felt this enormous—I don't know. I want to say connection."

I wanted her to say lust because that's what I wanted it to

be. "You wanted to see me again?" I asked.

"Yes. I feel like my head's spinning. I hardly slept last night. I'm really drawn to you. This is going to sound stupid, but it's like all of this happened so we'd meet."

She wore a white cashmere sweater that fit her snugly and some low-cut jeans that weren't bad either.

Our eyes locked. I had to make a decision fast because I was getting pretty hot. She made it for me. She leaned in and kissed me lightly on the lips. How fucking convenient that we were in a hotel room.

4

"My name's Valerie," she told me at one point. It was good to know because we were incredibly intimate.

"You must think I'm a horrible person," she said later when we were drinking the Sweetwater 420. We were undressed, sitting up on the bed.

I shook my head. I didn't know if she meant because she was having her husband killed, or because she'd jumped into bed with me, or because she was in bed with the person who was hired to kill her husband. I didn't care one way or the other. She was a freak in bed, and I was in heaven.

"I married too young," she said. "For the wrong reasons. He was unfaithful from the start. Then he turned abusive. It was a disastrous marriage. Now he won't divorce me."

Whatever. Maybe he was abusive. Maybe he wasn't. I didn't give a damn.

"I've begged him to let me go, but he won't."

I wanted to change the subject. "I went to Stone Mountain Park today."

This interested her. "Already?"

I put the beer in my left hand and laced my fingers through hers. "It's a cool place," I said.

"He goes almost every day. He might have been there

today."

"I'm going back tomorrow. I'll keep going until I see him, and it feels right."

She nodded like she understood. This assignment was turning out to be okay. I usually get bored on a job. One time I waitressed in Atlantic City for several weeks. I was so bored I thought about taking out a hit on myself. The target was the restaurant owner. He never knew who got him because I shot him from behind when he went out in a back alley for a smoke break. Anyway, this Atlanta job was going to be a piece of cake if I got to spend the week in bed with Valerie.

"It's really going to happen, isn't it?" she said more to herself than me. "Sometimes I don't know how I feel about him. I mean, I know I'm not in love with him. I never was. I just wish he would divorce me." She looked at me. "Are you Kelly?"

I brought her hand up to my mouth and sucked on her fingers. She didn't ask any more questions, and we messed around until we fell asleep.

My telephone woke us. It took me a while to find it in the pocket of the hoodie I'd thrown on the back of a chair.

"Were you asleep?" Rosa asked.

"No," I lied. I looked at the clock on the TV set. It was six o'clock in the evening.

"You sound like you were asleep."

"No. I'm a little stuffed up." I coughed. "They've got pollen here."

"Uh-huh." She didn't buy it. I glanced over at Valerie. She'd gotten out of bed and was putting on her clothes. I silently cursed Rosa.

"I'm serious," I said. "You can *see* it." This was true. There was yellow film on cars, sidewalks, everything. Still, it didn't seem to bother me. "Did you call for a reason?"

"Checking in," Rosa said.

Valerie picked up the beer bottles. I winced when they clinked together.

"Where are you?" Rosa asked.

"In a bar. Do you know you can't buy beer on Sundays? Except in a restaurant or bar?"

"You're joking."

"No. I wanted a beer, so I walked down the street."

Valerie was learning that I was an awful liar, but it was better than having Rosa find out I was entertaining the client in my hotel room. Holy Christ, she'd have a fucking fit.

"I went to the park today and plan to go back tomorrow," I said. "It's overwhelming. It's going to take me a while to get my bearings."

"That's what I figured. Is the weather good?"

"Beautiful."

"It sleeted here today," Rosa said with real pain in her voice.

"Sixty and sunny."

"Good for you. Enjoy your beer. I'll talk to you soon, sweetie."

"Are you hungry?" I asked Valerie after I hung up.

She was dressed and picking up her purse. Valerie moved like a thoroughbred. I wanted to fuck her again.

"I should go," she said with a grin. "I had a great time though."

"My boss wouldn't like this—" I pointed at her and then me.

"I won't tell."

That was a load off my mind.

"I could order room service," I said. "Or—"

"Not tonight, but can I see you tomorrow?"

"Absolutely."

I drove her back to Kroger. "Do you know where I can get a good pizza?" I asked, before she got out of the car.

She hesitated so long that I figured maybe pizza wasn't her

thing. She blinked and said, "Go down Peachtree that way." She pointed toward downtown Atlanta. "There's a pretty good pizza place on your left. Can't remember the name of it, but you'll see it."

"Thanks."

"I'll call you tomorrow. I had a great time. I really did."

"Me too."

We kissed, and she was gone. I followed Valerie's instructions and found the pizza place. I took a small pepperoni back to the hotel and watched HGTV. I ate the entire pizza and wished I still had some cake.

I called up the brokerage account on the laptop and checked my holdings. Things were looking fucking good.

5

There seemed to be a Waffle House on every Atlanta corner. The next morning I found one on the way to the park. I ate the cheese omelet, bacon, and hash browns again—still didn't want to try grits—and hit the road.

I cruised through the park gate after getting waved in by a different elderly woman. This lady blinked a lot and seemed to have problems with her eyes. If the majority of gate employees were this old and decrepit, I didn't need to worry about being identified.

It was Monday, and there were far fewer people at the park. I parked in the lot in front of the walking trail that led up the mountain. I was eager to climb it, but not today. Instead, I wanted to walk the sidewalk loop and scope out the trails.

It was another beautiful day. Sunny, cloudless, and mild. I had dressed for a workout in blue sweats and a red ball cap. My hair was tied back, and I wore shades. People were exceptionally friendly on the loop. It must be the weather because in Chicago you'd be lucky to get a terse nod. Many were African American. I wondered how they felt about the whole Confederacy theme.

I noticed something else. Frankly, many of the people I saw were overweight. I give them credit for coming out, trying to get into shape. However, if it came to a contest, I felt confident I could outrun everyone I saw. Easily.

Several emergency call boxes were placed maybe a mile apart. Two of them had signs on them: Out of Service. Not really important in this age of cell phones, but it gave me the idea that security wasn't an issue in the park.

I did see a number of police cars. This troubled me. Anytime I see one, I get chilled inside and out. Still, most of the black-and-whites were parked side by side at intersections. It looked like two bored cops talking to each other. I saw no flashing blue lights or anyone pulled over. I got the feeling that they were worried about speeders and loud music more than anything else. That was cool because I wasn't going to speed or crank the stereo.

Another thing I noticed. No security cameras. When I'd left the park the day before, I just drove out with no record of my entrance or exit. The poor saps were living in a time of innocence. Everything would change once I did the kill. They'd get cameras and more security. Maybe they'd let the ladies bring their own guns.

About halfway around the loop, I saw a white prison van. On one side of the road, orange jump-suited prisoners were laying pine straw while a uniformed guy who looked like a black Boss Hogg watched them. He had a gun secured in his holster, but he was lackadaisical and unthreatening.

The sidewalk's five miles were mostly even. There were a few small inclines, but nothing that got me breathing hard. It took a little more than an hour to walk the loop, but I wasn't trying to break any records. I figured I could run it in a half hour or so. Maybe tomorrow.

I returned to the parking lot and walked toward the mountain. I crossed railroad tracks and saw that the mountain was truly all one large rock except for some scrub pines and strange cactus-like plants. Most of it was exposed granite, making it look like the fucking moon. The climb was going to be fun. I planned to do it by the end of the week.

Something was bothering me. Well, a couple of things. One, I hadn't heard from Valerie. Two, I woke the previous night with the sudden fear that Mr. Kingsley had hired someone to follow his wife. She'd said that she was afraid he was on to her. If a private detective knew I'd met with her, the whole plan would have to be scrubbed. It would get done, just not here and not what we'd planned.

I drove back to Atlanta and showered. The phone rang when I was in the bathroom, and I checked my messages before I dressed. Valerie had called. My heart jumped when I heard the message.

"Hey, Lisa. This is Valerie. I'll try you later. Just wanted you to know I've been thinking about you."

I fist pumped the air. I could have called her back at the number that came up, but figured she had a good reason for not leaving a call back number. I needed to be smart.

True to her word, Valerie phoned again an hour later.

"Hey," she said, sounding relieved when I answered.

"I was in the shower when you called."

"Can I see you?"

I liked how she got to the point. "Absolutely."

"There's a Publix on Peachtree in the opposite direction of the Kroger," she said. "Pick me up there. It'll be on your right. I'll be in the beer aisle."

I left immediately, found her, and we headed back to the hotel with beer and sandwich fixings. The food was her idea, and it was fine with me.

"Is there any chance you're being followed?" I asked in the car.

She looked surprised. "I don't think so." Valerie twisted her body and looked out the back window. "Who'd be following us?"

"Could your husband have hired someone to keep an eye on you? You said you thought he knew something."

"No. He's not like that. We've been separated for three

years. We lead separate lives. I don't think he cares what I do. He lives with a woman. It's not like he's obsessed with me."

"Why do you think he knows—"

"I'm paranoid. I worry about it all the time." She shivered. "I just want it behind us."

Her use of the word "us" got to me. Us. She already thought of us as us. Cool. Sort of. It was flattering and terrifying at the same time. Wait—maybe she didn't mean me. I couldn't leave it alone. "Who's us?" I asked.

She blushed. "I just meant—Wow. I just—" She covered her mouth in a cute way.

"You get any other psychic feelings about me?" I asked, letting her off the hook.

"Yes."

I swallowed and waited. I don't even know if I believe in this stuff, but I have to admit that her so-called special powers made me feel funny.

"How long have you been psychic?" I asked.

"All my life." Valerie shook her head. "I knew not to marry him. Every time I haven't listened to my gut, I've regretted it. I've learned to pay attention to my instincts."

She didn't say another word until we got to my room. We both knew why we were there, so it wasn't long before we got down to business.

"This isn't something I'm overly familiar with," she said later. We were eating ham sandwiches on rye bread with mayo, mustard, and Romaine lettuce.

I kept my mouth shut and let her talk.

"I was raised in a strict atmosphere. My dad's German, and my mom's Cuban. I'm sure you can imagine what that was like."

I couldn't and wasn't interested enough to ask a follow-up question. I lit a joint for her. She nodded her thanks. This was another no-no. Rosa had always been strict about drug use on a job. I didn't give a fuck anymore.

"My parents came here to Atlanta to work in import-export," she said. "I was born here. They were having problems, so I got sent to European convent schools."

That was hot. "You have brothers and sisters?" I asked.

"Two sisters and a brother. All older. I feel incredibly drawn to you."

I hadn't paid close attention to everything she'd said, but this brought me back.

"There's something about you," she said. "Honestly, the first night we met, when you said, 'Mrs. Kingsley.'" She closed her eyes and moaned a little. "I don't know why or for how long, but I think we're supposed to be together. You must feel it too."

I smiled. I did, and I didn't. This was fun, but I wasn't sure how it could work long-term.

She chewed on a Ruffles potato chip and nodded at me. "Something happened to you when you were young. A tragic loss, but if it hadn't happened we wouldn't be together. Does that make any sense? It's like all roads lead to this."

I was creeped out. I was all for hearing about how we were meant to be together, but I didn't want to revisit my parents' deaths while lying naked in bed. We hadn't bothered to dress before making sandwiches because, really, what was the point? Anyway, some people might find this fine and dandy and be cool with it, but not me. I pretty much do an excellent job of not thinking about my parents.

Valerie saw something on my face because she leaned over and kissed me. "I'm sorry. I'll keep my psychic insights to myself. I will say this. I'm not worried anymore . Until I met you, I was a nervous wreck. Now I feel everything will be smooth sailing. Nothing can go wrong."

Like I said, I wasn't sure I believed in this shit. However, this relieved me tremendously.

"How long have you been doing this?" Valerie asked.

I tilted my head. She got the message.

"I guess you can't talk about it," she said. "Of course, you can't. That was stupid of—"

"A long time," I said, surprising myself.

She widened her eyes. "You're young. You must have been—How did you get involved in something like this? I keep asking questions you can't answer, don't I? I'm sorry."

"You're the first person I've wanted to tell. I'm not much of a talker. Sometimes I meet women on a job, but I don't—I don't usually open up this much."

"I can tell."

I chuckled. "I'll tell you something funny. When I first started doing this, I didn't know anything. I got a copy of a book. *Hit Man*. By a dude named Rex Feral."

Valerie was interested.

"The subtitle was *A Technical Manual for Independent Contractors.*"

"Did you learn anything from it?"

"A lot. One thing I learned was how to make a silencer."

"Will you use a silencer this—"

"Yes. But I don't make my own anymore. I buy 'em. I gotta tell you, Valerie. I wasn't very good at first. I got better. On my first job, I was walking down the street trying not to be suspicious, and I ran right into a parking meter. Almost knocked myself out."

Pretty soon we were laughing hard. It was a combination of the weed and the subject matter. Hilarious.

"You want to hear something else funny?" I was talking too much. It was stupid, but I didn't give a fuck. "One time I was supposed to do a job, and I stole some money. It made sense to make it look like a robbery." I shook my head. "The boss wasn't happy."

"Why?"

"It wasn't part of the contract. Guess what I had to do?"

"Take it back."

"Throw it away."

"You threw away money?"

"Cash. I threw it in a dumpster."

"How much?"

I shrugged. "A few thousand."

"Wow. Is she mean? Your boss?"

"No."

"She sounds mean."

"She's cool."

Valerie acted like she didn't believe me.

"She is." It was important that Valerie know I respected Rosa. "She's very cool. I love her. I don't love lots of people."

"Is she an ex?"

"It's complicated."

"Is she the one who got you started in this?"

I shrugged.

"Oh, I almost forgot," she said, putting her hand to her face. "I got you something." She grabbed her brown Michael Kors handbag and rooted through it. "Do you like chocolate?" she asked, glancing up at me.

"I love chocolate."

"Thought you might." Valerie brought out something from her purse and hid it with her body. She came back to the bed and handed me a white box. I took off the lid and saw a dozen small square chocolate pieces.

"It's chocolate toffee," Valerie said. "Like a Heath bar but—"

"I love Heath bars."

"It's a local company. Supposed to be really good."

I took a bite. "God, Valerie."

It was the best candy I'd ever tasted. Another sign. This woman knew my favorite candy without me telling her.

We fed each other the chocolate and spent the afternoon in bliss.

6

Valerie and I maintained the same schedule the next few days. In the morning, I ate at one of the many Waffle Houses and then went on my scouting mission. In the late morning, Valerie and I got together, and spent the rest of the day in the hotel room before we went our separate ways in the evening.

I climbed the mountain twice and was able to see all the way to Atlanta. I was winded the first time. The second time was easier. Next time, I thought to myself, I'll run up the damn thing. It was treacherous because the surface was slick. Some areas had loose gravel. I slipped a couple times, but it's not like I've never fallen on my ass.

I ventured beyond the sidewalk loop and hit the hiking trails, but still hadn't seen Hank Kingsley. This was fine. It was too soon. Hardly anyone used the trails. That was a relief. I might see someone every five minutes or so. In fact, I saw more deer than people. It was a trip to see them. I'd never hear them. Suddenly, they'd be there. I'd first think it was a dog. Once I realized what it was, I'd coo and baby talk. They'd dart off and disappear like magic.

The paths weren't totally isolated which troubled me. In many cases, the trail was within fifty feet of the sidewalk, and patches could be seen from the sidewalk loop. The hit was certainly not a piece of cake.

Valerie stopped talking about her psychic visions but shared information about her life. She told me she was thinking about going back to school.

"Everyone in my family has a degree," she said on the fourth day I was in town. "I feel like a loser. I went to Emory for a semester but dropped out when I married Hank."

"What were you studying?"

"Archaeology. I went on a dig in Charleston. Very cool." She smiled. "I wouldn't mind doing that again. I've thought about going into historic preservation. I like old houses. Did you go to school?"

"For a while, but I travel so much it got to be difficult. Guess what I studied?"

Valerie shrugged.

"Criminology."

She raised her eyebrows.

"Seriously. I did."

"Did it help?"

"No."

We laughed and kissed. I was falling for her. I was supposed to leave soon, but I was thinking about staying longer. Rosa wouldn't like it, but I wouldn't tell her that I'd fallen for the client. I'd make up something. I had no idea what I'd come up with, but I'd keep Valerie a secret.

Maybe, I thought to myself, maybe I could move to Atlanta. Valerie and I could live together, have a life. Eventually I'd have to tell Rosa, but she'd get over it. Maybe Valerie and I *were* supposed to be together.

"Do you get scared?" Valerie asked. "I would."

I thought about the question a long time. "I wouldn't use the word scared. Maybe in the beginning, but not now."

Last time I did a job for Rosa, things almost went real bad. I was supposed to knock off this rich guy who lived in a Gold

Coast condo. His wife hired me, and asked me to get him when he went on his daily stroll.

It was the dead of winter, and I wanted to get the thing over with. Unfortunately, I nearly offed an old, manly-looking woman who had the dumb luck to be walking outside. Rosa wasn't thrilled, and neither was I.

I finally got the dude, but it was a lot of work. Rosa got pissy and told me that she didn't think she'd have anything for me until spring.

"I've thought about going back to school," I said. Actually it had just occurred to me. I could move to Atlanta and take classes.

"Criminology again?"

"I don't think so. Maybe—" I thought for a long time. Valerie didn't become impatient. She seemed genuinely interested. "Psychology might be interesting."

"You want to become a counselor or—"

"No. Just interested in it."

"Do you know where you want to go? Somewhere in Chicago?"

I looked at her a long time. "Any good schools around here?"

"Emory is a great school. Just very expensive."

I smiled, letting her know that wasn't a problem. Valerie looked away, but I could have sworn that her eyes watered. I knew the look. She was falling for me big-time.

7

The Waffle House waitresses knew me by now. They were sweet and called me "hon" and "darling."

I'd finally asked one of them what grits tasted like. She looked at me like I was crazy. "You ain't never had grits, hon? She ain't never had grits!" She gave me a bowl of them—no charge—with my breakfast one morning. Grits weren't what I imagined them to be at all. They weren't bad, but I couldn't understand why you'd want them, especially if it was a choice between them and potatoes.

The same day that I tried grits I saw Hank Kingsley. It was my sixth day in Atlanta. I walked onto the trail about nine in the morning. I was on it for fifteen minutes when I heard twigs and leaves crunching and caught sight of someone coming toward me. I thought, I wonder if it's him. Valerie's psychic ability must have rubbed off on me because it was.

A smallish guy, he wore a blue windbreaker and a Georgia Tech baseball cap. The trail was narrow, so when we passed we almost touched. One of us had to give and turn sideways. Apparently a gentleman, Hank did it for me. He walked fast, obviously in a hurry or enjoying a brisk workout. I'd looked at his photograph enough times that I had no doubt it was him.

"Morning," we said simultaneously.

I turned and winked at him after he passed. I had the gun with me, but I wasn't ready.

My adrenalin pumping, I headed back to the sidewalk and went into a full throttle run. The next time I saw him, maybe tomorrow, I might kill him.

"I saw him on the trail just now." I said to Rosa when I called her from the car in the parking lot. "I'll see if he keeps the same schedule tomorrow."

"Sounds good, sweetie."

"Did you ever tell the wife anything about me?"

"Like what?"

"Anything."

"No. Of course not."

Of course not. I knew that.

"Why?" she asked.

"Just curious." I had to make up something. "She didn't seem surprised I was a woman."

"I didn't say anything to her about you other than that you were the best, that she wouldn't have anything to worry about. I didn't mention gender. You haven't talked to her again, have you?"

"No," I lied. "I guess she thinks we're going about our business. Have you heard from her?"

"Not since the day you got there. I assumed you reassured her."

"I tried."

"You bored yet?"

"You know me."

Rosa chuckled. "I do know you. You're thinking it'll be tomorrow?"

"Maybe."

There was a long silence before Rosa spoke again. "Is it me, or does this one seem like it's taking a long time?"

"Fort Lauderdale took a while."

"That's true."

The Fort Lauderdale kill had happened the previous winter. I was hired to kill the ex-lover of movie star Gary Powers. His ex had been blackmailing him for years, and GP, as everyone calls him, had finally had it. The ex had a roommate, so I had to make sure that she was out of the apartment before I did it. The whole thing finally worked out, but I liked the Florida weather and stayed on for a while until Rosa called me home for another job. I hooked up with a friendly girl who turned out to have an addiction problem. When I left, I put a bunch of cash under her pillow and hoped she'd use it to pay bills. I never talked to her again.

I debated whether to tell Valerie I'd seen her husband. Part of me feared she'd freak out and change her mind. I was doing the hit soon. I didn't need complications. I decided not to tell her. I told myself it was because of professionalism, but it was because I didn't know how she'd react.

The next day it rained. Hard. A steady stream of hard pellets. No one would be at the park. That was the bad news. The good news was that Valerie called around nine, and we got together an hour later. She brought pot with her. I thought that was all right.

"I saw him yesterday on the trail," I said, surprising myself. Maybe it was the weed. We'd been going at it so long my lips were bruised, and my cherry was sore. *Every time a dyke comes, an angel gets its wings.* That was another of Rosa's sayings. Lots of angels got their fucking wings that morning, buddy.

She sat up quickly. "You saw him?"

I nodded.

"You didn't—"

"No." I shook my head. "It's got to be right. Soon," I promised.

She took a deep breath and eased back down. I wanted to tell her that I'd been thinking about us being together, that I might move to Atlanta. What would she think of that? If she was so damn psychic, she ought to know, shouldn't she?

"You're not going to leave right away, are you?" she asked. "Afterwards. Please tell me you're not."

I avoided the question. "You'll be investigated. Make sure you have an alibi when I'm at the park."

She nodded and cleared her throat. "Will you go back to Chicago immediately?"

I shrugged.

"Lisa." She had a serious look. "Do you think of this as a fling, something to do while you're here? I need to know. I gotta tell you, I'm falling for you."

I tongue kissed her hard and looked into her eyes. "I have never done anything like this before. I'm falling for you too. I've told you things I've never told anyone. There's more things I want to tell you."

"Promise you won't leave after you do it. See me again. Will you promise? We'll figure out everything else after that, but please don't leave."

"I promise."

The next day I drove to the park. I'd made up my mind that this would be the day. The sun had returned. It felt cleansing. In fact, the powdery pollen had washed away, except for a few small yellow puddles.

I was on the trail for ten minutes when I saw Hank coming toward me. I'd wait for him to pass, glance around to make sure no one was in sight, and shoot the fucker in the back.

I patted the gun under my jacket. He was within ten feet of me when I realized with a sickening jolt that he had a dog on a leash. It might not be bad luck to kill a man with a dog, but it should be. Fucking fuck.

41

"Morning," he said. He smiled like he recognized me.

He had a small gray and white dog. Cute little bouncy thing, who, I swear, grinned at me. I was so fucking frustrated I wanted to scream after they passed.

"He had a dog with him," I told Valerie later that morning when we were at my hotel.

She looked puzzled.

"A little dog," I said.

"What kind?"

"I don't know. A little gray and white thing."

"A guard dog?"

"No. A lap dog." I gave her a look. "Everything's off if he has a dog."

Her mouth dropped open.

"I'm not going to hurt a dog," I said. "The dog will start barking. Create a commotion. Then what am I going to do with the dog?"

I was amped up, raging a bit. She hadn't seen this side of me. It's not attractive. I ran my hands through my hair.

"Did you know he had a dog?" I asked.

"I don't know anything about a dog."

"Maybe it's his girlfriend's dog."

"Maybe. We didn't have a dog. I don't want you to hurt the dog."

"Good. Because I'm not going to."

I didn't tell her about my childhood dogs. They were good boys. My dad brought home two little terrier-mix puppies from a shelter when I was young. I'm not sure why he brought home two. He said something about how they could be companions to each other. I think he was soft-hearted and fell in love with both of them. Mom must have known because she wasn't mad at all. She gushed when he brought them in. I named them Chili and Pizza because those were my favorite foods. They slept in my bed. The dogs weren't related, but they acted like brothers until they died of old age within a month of each other. There were lots of tears in the house. Dad said something about getting new dogs, but it never happened. A year later, Mom and Dad were dead, and I was the only surviving Digby.

Anyway, this was the first day Valerie and I saw each other and didn't have sex. I was rattled. If Hank came to the park with a dog again, I'd have to find a different place to kill him. I'd spent a fucking week getting this thing set up and wasn't looking forward to starting over.

"I don't know why he came with a dog," she said. "I don't think it'll be a regular thing."

"I hope not. Because I'll have to kill him somewhere else. It won't work with a dog."

She put up her hands. She thought I was overreacting. Maybe I was. I hate when things don't go smoothly. She didn't stay much longer. I drove her to Kroger, dropped her off, and went back to the hotel alone. We didn't kiss goodbye.

Rosa calmed me down when I called. "All right, Kell, if he brings the dog next time, we'll come up with plan B. I know you've got a thing about Chili and Pizza. No one wants you to hurt a dog. Shake it off. Plans change. It happens. Go do something fun. Get a facial or something."

"That's your idea of fun."

"Have a date with one of your Waffle House gals."

"Bless their hearts," I said with a southern accent, "they don't have a full set of teeth between them."

Rosa laughed. "You sound agitated. Relax. This too shall pass. It's a minor setback. Want me to find the address of a dyke bar?"

"No. I'll be fine."

"It wouldn't hurt you to go out and blow off some steam. Maybe bring someone back to the hotel."

"I'll be okay. I just wish it was over."

"Me too."

Valerie called me less than five minutes after I hung up with Rosa. "Things seemed tense between us," she said. "I don't like it. This is a stressful time. I'm sorry if you thought I was giving you a hard time. I wasn't. Not at all. I'm on your side, baby. I want to see you. I'm at the Barnes & Noble down the street. Will you come get me?"

I was glad she called. Rosa was right. I needed to relax. "I had it in my head that it was going to happen today, and it didn't," I explained as we drove back from the Barnes & Noble.

"I understand." She squeezed my hand.

Once back in the hotel room, we quickly undressed and screwed around on the bed. It was exactly what I needed. I'd started having doubts about staying with Valerie, but now I realized that I wanted to stay in Atlanta. We might have to move somewhere else, but I'd tell Rosa I was done. She'd fuss, but I was feeling more and more that I had to get out of this life.

I didn't tell any of this to Valerie, but I could see us staying together for a long time. We'd had our first fight, and it was all right. Things were going to be fine. I was stressed. It would be over soon.

8

I slept well and drove to the park the next morning. If Hank had the dog again, I wouldn't like it, but I'd come up with Plan B. If he didn't have the dog, I'd do it. Then I'd worry about what I was going to tell Rosa about staying with Valerie.

He didn't have the dog, but I didn't do it. I can't say why exactly, but I didn't go through with it. I saw him, got a feeling that something wasn't right, and let him pass. We nodded at each other. He smiled. I grimaced.

Valerie stared at me when I told her. She thought I'd lost my nerve.

"I thought you said if he didn't have the dog—"

"Everything's got to be right. Something felt off today." If I hadn't met Valerie, Hank Kingsley would be dead now. She'd definitely thrown me off my game. I couldn't blame her really, but I did. "It's going to happen. Soon."

She looked doubtful. Still, we had sex. She was rough this time. She pinned me and kissed and rubbed me hard. Truth to tell, I didn't mind. Kind of spiced things up a bit, if you know what I mean.

"I was thinking," she said later, "have you ever killed more than one person to get the heat off of you?"

"I don't get you."

"Let's say you kill some stranger in the park. Then you kill the guy you're supposed to kill. The police would think it was a serial murderer. Not that he was the target."

"First," I said, beginning to wonder about her, "it's not easy to kill someone. It takes planning, and even then something can go wrong. Second, if I kill someone at the park, there'd be cops all over the place. I guess it might work if the bodies were found around the same time. It wouldn't look like one was particularly targeted, but—"

Awareness spread over her features. "You're right. I hadn't thought about that."

I knew what was really on her mind. "You'll have an alibi," I said. "It will be an unsolved murder."

"Has anyone ever been charged with one of yours?"

That was a good question. I honestly didn't know the answer. "Never the client."

"Sometimes innocent people get charged? I wonder if anyone ever got executed." She didn't seem upset, just curious.

"I suppose it might have happened. After I leave, I don't know."

"Have you ever killed more than one person at the same time?"

"Yes."

"Accidentally or—"

"*Accidentally?* Give me a break. I'm a professional. I don't do collateral damage. I've been hired to kill two people at the same time. Usually a husband and wife."

She thought about this a long time. I started talking before she had time to come up with a question. "One time it was real easy because they were drug addicts. Pop. Pop. They were on something, and it was easy to get in the house, easy to get to them. They actually smiled when they saw me, saw the gun."

"Who hired you?" she asked after a long silence.

"The woman's husband."

"That's what it mainly is, isn't it? Love that's turned."

"My boss says it's love or money or both. One time this dude who looked like Steve Buscemi hired me to kill his ex-business partner and ex-wife—"

"Ooh."

"Yeah. That one wasn't easy. Anyway, the marriage and business had gone bust ten years before. The guy waited *ten years* to get them."

"Is it harder to kill a woman?"

"Not this one. She was a real bitch."

I got the feeling that Valerie wanted me to say it was harder to kill a woman, but I wanted her to get to know the real me.

The next day was cold. The temperature dropped into the forties, the sky was overcast, and a blustery wind blew. A perfect day for killing. Hank never had a chance. It wasn't just because he didn't have the dog, or the wind made me meaner. He never saw me as a threat. He'd seen me on the trail a few times, and I'm a pretty girl. No one tenses up, goes on the defensive when they see me. The only better disguise would be one of the elderly gatekeepers at the park entrance. That gave me a tremendous idea, maybe because I was feeling guilty about quitting on Rosa. She should hire old lady hit men. I know they wouldn't have great physical strength, but if they could be trained to shoot a gun, well, they'd make great professionals. Anyway, my point is that I see both men and women ease up when they see me. No one suspects in a million years that I'm a hit man.

I had another piece of luck. Hank was listening to an MP3 player. The dude actually had buds in his ears.

"Morning," I said.

He nodded, but probably never heard my greeting. We passed. I stopped after five feet, glanced around, slid out the gun, crept up behind him, effortlessly aimed where I knew it'd do the most damage, gathered up his fallen body by the coat collar, dragged it ten feet into the overgrowth, and dumped him next to a thick, rotting trunk. It took me only a few frantic seconds to find the shell casing. It'd fallen next to a sapling a few feet off the trail. I scooped it up and continued walking. I didn't see another person until I made it onto the sidewalk.

"Morning," I said to two smiling, pleasant black women.

I drove about an hour east until I cruised into Athens, home of the Georgia Bulldogs. I stopped and ate at the Varsity drive-in on Broad Street. A cute and goofy car hop with purple hair, probably a college student, brought my food. She giggled a lot and brought me a couple chili dogs, onion rings, and a frosted orange. After I ate, I went inside to the bathroom and changed my clothes. I left the Varsity and went to a thrift store a couple blocks away. I donated my shoes, socks, jeans, shirt, jacket, and cap. The middle-aged, red haired lady at the thrift store was thrilled and gave me a tax slip. Some lucky college student would soon be wearing a hit man's clothes, and I was going to get a tax deduction. Is this a great country or what?

I got back on the road and turned on my phone. Valerie had left two messages.

"Lisa, I'll try again later," was the first.

The second was a little different. "Hey, Lisa. I hope I get a chance to talk to you soon."

I called Rosa.

"Everything okay?" she asked.

"Splendid."

There was silence for a moment. "Stay a couple days and then come home."

"Okay," I said, though I wasn't sure I was coming home.

"I love you, Kell."

What in the world was going on with Rosa? She'd never been this lovie-dovie. "I love you too, Rosa. We need to talk when I get back."

"I'd like that very much."

I wasn't sure that she'd like it all that much. I waited for Valerie to call again. I drove back to the hotel and waited some more. I got panicky when I hadn't heard from her at dinnertime. I turned on the local news in my room. Nothing on the murder.

It got late. By ten p.m., I was going crazy. Maybe Valerie had played with me. He was dead. What use did she have for me now? Maybe she got hot thinking I was going to kill him. Maybe it was a game, and the game was over.

I wanted to call her, but knew it was dumb. What if they'd found the body, and she was being questioned? Her phone goes off, and it's stupid me?

It got to be midnight. I went out and bought a pack of cigs. Do you have any idea how expensive they are now? Holy fuck. Six dollars a pack? You've got to be fucking kidding me.

I was in a no-smoking room, but fuck that. I sat on the bed with the lights on and smoked one after the other. They tasted horrible and made me cough. Fucking wimp, I taunted myself.

I kept my clothes on, hoping Valerie would call. Did she know it was done? She claimed to be intuitive, after all. Why didn't she call? For God's sake, she wanted it done. Didn't she? I drifted off a few times. A half hour here. An hour there.

Finally, it was morning. I was afraid to take a shower, fearing I'd miss her call. I went down to the lobby and bought a newspaper. Nothing about Hank.

I went back up to my room and turned the TV to a local station.

They'd found Hank. The channel showed footage of the park. It was a fucking madhouse. Helicopters, cop cars, most of the park blocked off.

They put up a picture of Hank and described him as a forty-two year old Atlanta nightclub owner. A woman who was walking her dog had discovered him.

Something puzzled me. The anchor said Kingsley was unmarried. TV stations get a lot of things wrong. Still, it was something I wanted to ask Valerie about.

I couldn't eat. I didn't want to walk down to Waffle House because I didn't want to chat and smile and act like nothing was wrong. I got in the car and found a Starbucks a few blocks from the hotel. I got a fancy caramel coffee. I thought about getting a pastry but wasn't hungry. Rosa told me to stay a couple days, but I went back to the hotel and packed. Maybe it was smarter to leave and then reconnect with Valerie when things cooled down. By the time I'd convinced myself to return to Chicago, the phone rang. It was her.

9

"Hey, Lisa." Valerie sounded weird, almost like she'd been drugged. "I've heard some horrible news."

She was worried the conversation was being taped. It was a legitimate concern. If she was paranoid before, it was really going to kick in now.

"Yeah. I heard about it too. I'm really sorry."

"Yeah. A fucking senseless tragedy." Valerie sighed. "I decided to go up to my cabin in the mountains. North Georgia. It's about an hour away. Why don't you come up? I'll give you directions. I could use some moral support."

There was a different tone in her voice. Something had changed. Yeah, her husband was dead, but it seemed that something else was different too. I couldn't put my finger on it, but I got the feeling that it wasn't good for me. I should have driven back to Chicago, but wanted to hear the kiss off, if that's what it was.

"Let's take a break and see how we feel when the dust has settled," I said aloud when I was driving. "Too much has happened. I need time to think." Valerie might go with something like that. With any luck, she'd agree to have sex with me one last time. I'd go back and tell Rosa some of it. Not all of it. She'd say, "Poor baby got her heart broken." I'd forget about it after a while. Maybe Valerie would call in a few months. I'd tell myself I was over it, and then drive back to Atlanta. I was so sick of my stupid heart I wanted to smack my face against the steering wheel.

I turned on the radio and listened to the local news. The murder was big. No one had been murdered in the park before. A reporter said it looked like a gangland hit.

Valerie's detailed directions were great which was good because the GPS came up blank when I plugged in the address. The fucking maps needed to be updated. Her place was off the interstate, and it took more than an hour to get there. I had to drive two-lane country roads with ridiculous speed limits. It was a part of Georgia I never knew existed. Rural and pretty. Dense hills of towering pine trees and hardwoods, totally unlike the ubiquitous farmers' fields in rural Illinois.

I drove down two dirt roads before I got to Valerie's street. It was in a remote area, but not totally desolate. I saw at least two other houses within a few hundred yards of Valerie's. She called her place a cabin, but it was a substantial A-frame wood house. I recognized her Lexus SUV sitting alone in the driveway and pulled over before I reached it.

Rosa had always told me to trust my gut. Something was up. I heard a buzzing sound in my head, only there wasn't any sound, and it wasn't in my head. I wouldn't say that I was afraid. I would say I was on heightened alert. That's what Rosa had called it. "Be on heightened alert." She'd also said, "If you ever feel uncomfortable about something, if it doesn't feel right, get the hell out." I'd followed her advice before. I didn't this time. Maybe I was curious. Maybe I had a death wish.

I got out of the car and quietly closed the door. I took an angle and walked to the side of the house and then headed to the back. I was tingly, wondering if someone already had me in their sights.

The screen door was shut, but the wooden back door was

open, revealing an empty kitchen. I carefully opened the screen door and stepped inside. The kitchen was small with new-looking black appliances. A royal blue towel hung on the oven handle. For a moment, I was rooted, listening. I heard nothing. I took a couple steps and looked through the doorway that led to the front room.

Valerie stood with her back against the wall on one side of the front door. With two hands, she held a gun at her waist. She was in a great position to blast whoever stepped through the front door. I was in no man's land. She hadn't seen me, but any movement would alert her. I had few options. If I rushed her, I had little chance of overpowering her before she fired. If I turned and ran, she'd easily shoot me in the back. I wanted to laugh. I was a fucking idiot. I didn't have a fucking gun because I'd left it in the backpack in the car.

Valerie saw me. Her panicked eyes widened. In slow motion, she raised the gun and pointed it at my face. When she closed her eyes, I went down to my knees and saw a flash. Rosa had once told me that if someone was shooting at my head to drop to the ground. With any luck, the timing would be just right, and the bullet would go over my head. Then I could charge the shooter.

Valerie was a poor marksman. The bullet grazed the left side of my head, taking a fair bit of skin with it. It burned like hell. Someone shrieked. I charged and pounced on her, easily taking her down.

Valerie was lucky she hadn't blown off her own beautiful face. She wasn't a pro. It's so important to hire a professional for these kinds of things. Rosa had always said that. Goddamn fucking Rosa had cheaped out.

10

"Who was Hank Kingsley?" I asked through my teeth. My heart was beating fast. Valerie was gasping, making weird squeaky noises.

"I don't know."

"Who was he?" I grabbed a handful of hair and pulled her face closer to mine.

"I don't know!"

My mind click-clacked. I saw the whole fucking picture. I wanted to beat myself up for being so dumb.

"When did you meet Rosa?" I asked.

Valerie tried to roll up in a protective ball. She was terrified. She ought to be. She'd tried to kill me, was unsuccessful, and now had to deal with me. I'd be scared too. I pulled back my fist, letting her know I'd smash her if she didn't say something. She talked.

"About four months ago," she said.

"Where?"

"Las Vegas."

I thought for a moment. The last time Rosa went to Vegas was around Thanksgiving. She'd told me when she returned that she'd broken even. "Made enough to pay for my flight and hotel. Not a bad time." She'd never mentioned meeting anyone or celebrating fucking St. Lisa's Day.

"Whose idea was this?" I asked, though I knew. Valerie wasn't a half-brain, but she also wasn't Rosa. She wouldn't tell me, even when I threatened again to hit her. That was commendable. She was protecting Rosa. Loyalty is important. Too bad she'd given it to Rosa and not me.

I held the gun on Valerie while I rummaged in drawers and cabinets. She was lying on her side, facing the wall, crying. I found twine and tied her. I wasn't gentle. She offered no resistance. She'd given up.

I didn't have a lot to work with, so I had to make do. I shoved her in a walk-in closet and laid her flat. Then I duct taped her to the floor and walls, head to foot. She couldn't move, and it wasn't going to be a Sunday school picnic when someone released her. Before I stuffed her mouth with a sock, she pleaded with me. "Please. Don't. Not in here. Please. I'm begging you. I'm afraid of the dark."

"You shouldn't have played with Rosa and me," I said to her horrified, widened eyes. I crammed a sock into her mouth, put another piece of duct tape over it, and taped it across the carpet floor and onto the wall. Then I did it a few more times. It was going to be a fucking mess trying to get her out of this tape prison. I turned off the light and shut the closet door. Frantic, muffled grunts came through the door. Tough.

I wanted to get back to Illinois as soon as possible. I had business to attend to. I couldn't take a plane because it was too much of a hassle to fly, especially for a hit man. What about a train? What the fuck did I know about trains? I'd drive. Yeah, it would take a long time, but it was my only choice.

I peeled out of North Georgia and sped towards Chicago. I felt invisible. I was going ninety to one hundred miles an hour and never saw one cop. Maybe I'm dead, I thought. Maybe the bitch killed me. I touched the side of my head. It was bleeding and sore. Flesh was gone, destroyed. It hurt like hell. I must be alive.

A long time ago, I asked Rosa what she was going to do when I was too old to work for Ironclad. "I guess we'll have to kill you, sweetie." We laughed. It wasn't so fucking funny now.

The drive back to Illinois was eerie. I stopped twice for gas. I didn't eat, pee, or drink either time. One time I stood at a pump in Tennessee while a carful of punks shouted crude comments at me. Apparently it wasn't unusual for them to see an attractive woman with a fairly serious head wound in jeans and a University of Miami hoodie pumping gas. The hoodie was too large. I'd grabbed it out of a drawer at the cabin because I was cold and needed to cover up my blood-stained sweater.

I thought about pulling out my gun and shooting them all dead. It was a stupid idea, one that came from a dark, rage-filled hole. Killing them would slow me down, not to mention guarantee I'd have cops following me.

I got to Glencoe in a little less than ten hours. It didn't seem that long. I wondered if anyone had found Valerie yet. If not, those ten hours had been brutal for her. Too fucking bad.

I didn't want Rosa to see my car, so I parked it a few houses away, down at the Schulman's. They spent the winter months in Florida and weren't due back until May. Still, I was taking a chance. Someone might see the car and report it as suspicious. That's the kind of neighborhood Rosa lived in. Safe.

Rosa's house had all kinds of security measures. I knew all of them, plus the codes. I even had all the keys. Unless she'd changed everything after I left. She might have done that. I came up on the side of the garage and looked in the window. The Jaguar was gone. She wasn't home.

My key worked in the back door. Once in the kitchen, I punched in the code for the security system. It took it.

I went through the house, room by room. She might have already left for Atlanta. She could be there now. Maybe that was the plan. To meet in Atlanta after the hit on me. The idea that I might not be able to confront her made me want to cry. I was primed for a fight.

Her laptop was still set up on her bedroom desk. When she traveled, she always took it. Relieved, I went back downstairs and touched the PC's mouse on the countertop in the kitchen. It brought up the screen.

Satisfied she'd return, I gulped several glasses of water from the refrigerator door dispenser. Water dribbled down my chin and onto the floor. I wiped at the puddle with my blood-spattered shoes.

I had time to waste, so I went into the powder room off the kitchen and looked in the mirror. I looked fucking calm. It was like the person inside me and the person looking in the mirror were two different people.

The head wound had stopped bleeding. Dried, caked blood darkened and clumped my hair. My lips were dry and chapped. My skin was pale. I'd looked better.

I went back to the kitchen and stood in front of the computer. I clicked on the icon that took me online. I wanted to get into Rosa's email account. A message came up asking for a password.

I tried different passwords. Nothing worked. I even tried Lisa Bruce and Valerie. I clicked on the icon that took me to Rosa's accounting program. It, too, asked for a password. Just when I was about to pick up the fucking computer and throw it across the goddamn room, I heard the garage door open.

I waited behind the door that led from the garage to the kitchen. Rosa came in, carrying two grocery bags from Trader Joe's. A wine bottle peeked out the top of one. She set the bags on the counter. Her back was to me.

"Are we celebrating something?" I asked.

She whirled and stared. Her face drained of blood. She tried to control her breathing. After a long silence, she asked, "What happened to your head? Are you all right?"

I shook my head. "It's nothing. You should see the other guy."

She took a step back, but it took her into the granite counter. Still, she tried to step back again. Rosa gripped her hands against the counter, bracing herself. "What happened?"

"You know what happened. I could ask you why, but you'd make up something. We both know the reason is money. It's the money, honey. And love."

She shook her head. "You're wrong," she said, but wasn't convincing. She looked me over, trying to figure out where my gun was. I could tell by the look on her face that I didn't need to point a gun at her to get her to do what I asked.

"Kell, let's—"

I put my finger to my lips. She stopped talking. I nodded toward the computer. "Open up the books for me."

She helplessly looked at her groceries and back at me. "Kell—"

I again put a finger to my lips. She walked to the computer.

"What's the password?" I asked. "I couldn't get in."

She placed her shaking hands over the keyboard. She started to type, but the trembling made her make mistakes.

"What's the password?" I asked again.

"Your name, first name, all caps, and your birth year," she mumbled.

I wanted to believe her, but figured it was a lie to flatter me. I watched as she typed. It turned out to be true.

"You owe me one hundred grand for this job. Transfer the money into my checking account." She did it within a minute. I watched what she'd done and got a feel for the software. "Show me the amount of life insurance you had on me."

Rosa put her hands in her lap. "Kell, I—"

"Show me!"

"It wasn't about that."

"Shut-the-fuck-up-and-show-me."

She pulled up a page that was a profile on me. It had my name, address, social security number, birth information, health insurance, and bank account number. I examined it carefully. It had crossed my mind that she might have been cheating me all these years. She'd told me early on that she'd changed my commission to make us fifty-fifty. Under a heading titled Commission was 50%. Good. Under the Life Insurance column was this information: $2 million—Company Paid.

"Transfer two million into my brokerage account," I said.

Rosa sighed. "I gotta tell you, kid. I have to do it as income. This is going to kill you on taxes."

"Do it."

She did. It took a few minutes. She finished the transaction and waited for my next instruction. I was proud of her for not begging. I would have been disappointed if she'd gone all hysterical on me.

"Run a report and show me what the company netted the last three years." I'd thought about this while I waited for her to return. It was a fair estimate of my value to her.

She put her fingers on the keyboard, but took them off.

"Don't tell me you don't know how to do it, Rosa."

"It's not that. It's—" Her voice trailed off.

"I don't care what it is!" I sounded crazy even to myself. My voice was out of control. "Fucking do it, bitch!" I'd never called her a name in my life, not even in joking.

She typed a few commands. A page came up that showed expenses and income for the previous three years. I stared at it until I understood it. "I want two point five million to go into my brokerage account." This was half of the net. She had a few other people working for her, but I'd done most of the work. Rosa didn't move for several moments. "I don't care what you have to transfer or liquidate. Do it and transfer two point five million dollars into my fucking account."

This took Rosa longer. I watched as she sold stocks and

mutual funds. I could tell it was painful. One time she stopped, seemingly torn between selling off Fundamental Investors or Small Cap World Fund Class A.

"I am losing my fucking patience."

She sold off Fundamental Investors. Finally, I watched as she transferred another $2.5 million into my account.

"Who did I kill?" I asked.

"Hank Kingsley."

"Valerie wasn't the client?"

"No."

"Who was?"

She waved her hand. "It's complicated." Her head went down. Her eyes stared at the keyboard. She clasped her hands in front of her. She figured the transactions were over.

"You wanted one last job from me," I said.

"I wish you'd let me explain." Her head stayed down. Like Valerie, she'd given up.

I stood behind her several minutes wondering how to say goodbye. My chest was heavy and tight, like something was trying to get out. I couldn't think of anything to say. "Your girlfriend is tied up in her closet at the cabin. If she hasn't been found yet, she's been there for almost twelve hours. You probably want to do something about that." My voice broke on the last sentence.

She turned and shot me the saddest look. "Baby" is all she said. I didn't know if she meant me or Valerie. I left.

PART II

11

I returned the fucking rental to the Enterprise lot on Kedzie, picked up the Mustang, and drove to my condo. For all I knew, Rosa had already hired someone else to take me out. I moved the sofa, a chest of drawers, and a desk in front of the door.

Before I took a shower, I steeled myself to look closely at the head wound. It was a sticky mess. I carefully wiped at it until I could see how deep and wide it was. It wasn't pretty, but it was essentially a flesh wound. It was a miracle no bone had been hit. Still, the injury was going to scar. If I'd gone to a doctor, I would have been given something that would have lessened that, but there's no way I could explain a bullet wound, and they wouldn't have been able to stitch anything because the flesh was gone.

I'd been lucky. If Valerie had pointed a little to the left, the bullet would have penetrated my skull and hit brain. Death or a drooling idiot the rest of my diapered life.

I had a headache like I'd been hit with a hammer. I wanted to drive back to Glencoe, put my head in Rosa's lap, and cry at her feet. "Bitch shot me in the *head*, Rosa!"

After my shower, I sat at the computer and checked my bank account and portfolio. The funds were still there. I changed my passwords to make it difficult for Rosa. A terrible realization hit me. Rosa had put my portfolio together. She'd set up everything and picked the mutual funds. Guess who the beneficiary was? She not only would have gotten my life insurance and the payment for the Kingsley hit, she would have won the big prize. My entire fucking portfolio. I was the pig she'd fattened to take to market.

The next few weeks were lost ones. I didn't work out and ate little. I ignored most voice and emails, except for Joy and Mary. I'd occasionally had sex with both of them, though not at the same time. I felt like I owed them a little more, so I sent them terse texts that I was busy with work and unavailable.

I finally moved the furniture away from the door, figuring that death by a hit man wouldn't be all that bad. I unpacked.

I cried a lot too. More than I'd ever done in my life. These were sobs that took hold of me, made me whimper and squeal. I'd turned into a teenage girl.

I checked my accounts every day. They still had all the money. Once a week, I changed my passwords.

I hadn't heard from Rosa. You probably think it strange I didn't want to kill her. I had no revenge fantasies. The anger gave way to a sadness so big it felt like it was inside and outside of me.

We'd played a game. Rosa had won. If I hurt her because of it, then I was a big fucking baby. Something clicked every day. I wanted to box myself in the head for being so dumb. The reason Valerie was in a hurry to get the hit over with was so she could stop fucking me and be with Rosa. That cute little bit when she threw away my name and phone number at the food court? Rosa had already given her my number, not to mention my name and background details. She'd even told her what perfume I liked, my favorite candy, what I preferred in bed. They were in constant communication, planning what to do next, based on what I'd done, how I'd reacted.

It was genius to give Valerie the psychic "gift." Years ago, shortly after I became a hit man, I got it in my head that I wanted to see a medium. I hoped to connect with my parents. Rosa discouraged me, telling me that I'd be exploited. I think she worried that I might get religion. She also worried that a genuine psychic might ask too many questions. Anyway, I never went, and I also decided that when a person dies, that's it. You were alive or you were dead. Two options. This, as you might imagine, was comforting to someone like me.

Some things still didn't make sense. How in the hell had I mistaken Valerie's kindness for pity? Why had Rosa cooked for me and slept with me before sending me to my death? Why had she told me she loved me and talked about living together? Guilt? Why had she decided to get rid of me? Was Valerie my replacement? If she was, she'd make a pathetic hit man. Did Rosa hate me? When did she decide to kill me? Had I said or done something? "When you figure out women, Kell, come and tell me all about it," Rosa used to say. Wasn't that the fucking truth?

I needed to move away from Chicago. I could afford to live anywhere I wanted. I started looking at real estate online. I checked out places like Hawaii and San Francisco. I even looked into living in France, but discarded that idea since I can't speak French and didn't want to fucking learn.

I kept thinking about Atlanta. The weather had been great in March. It was a beautiful city, and I'd fallen in love with that stupid park, even if it was a Confederate memorial. The cost of living was low. The only negative was the stupid alcohol law on Sundays. It wasn't like I'd run into Valerie. For all I knew, she was living with Rosa in Glencoe.

I looked at property online in the Stone Mountain area. I specifically looked for something near the park for less than a million. After looking for a couple weeks, I found a gem in an area called Smokerise. It was listed for $499,000 and included all furnishings. Less than a mile from the park, it seemed perfect. I called a puzzled real estate agent and offered $450,000. A few weeks later, after a little back and forth, I bought the house and furnishings for $459,000.

I leased my Chicago condo to a friend of Mary's, and moved to Georgia a month later. It was a great house, a two-story brick with back and front staircases, and a glass sunroom. Still, I didn't know what I was getting myself into. Summer in Georgia was hotter than I thought possible, and the bugs were terrible. I stayed inside most of the time, except for visiting a package store not far from the house. I slept a lot, under tons of heavy blankets, with the blinds drawn and the air conditioner cranked.

When I wasn't sleeping, I was drunk and eating antidepressants. Years ago, I'd dated a pharmaceutical rep who'd given me bags of Prozac, Xanax, and tons of other stuff I couldn't even pronounce. Eventually, I'd run out of samples and have to find a doctor to get more. I dreaded that.

I went on a booze run one day and noticed my grass was long, especially compared to the neighbor's. I'd never had to worry about mowing at my condo. I didn't even own a lawn mower. On my way back, I saw a chick trimming a neighbor's hedges. I pulled my Mustang to the curb. A big black Tundra with the name Floratropolis Garden and Design on the side of the door was parked in the driveway. I assumed it was the chick's. She wore a straw hat and had her back to me. She didn't turn when I stopped the car.

"Excuse me!" I yelled.

She turned. She wore earbuds and pulled one out, warily eyeing me.

The chick had a mass of long curly blonde hair, tied back. She was tan. Pretty buff too. She was sweating, but so was I, just sitting in the car. It must have been a hundred degrees.

She nodded for me to continue.

"Do you mow lawns?" I asked.

She hesitated. "I have," she finally said.

It occurred to me that I might be talking to the owner of the house. It was weird the way she'd said, "I have." I was thrown off.

"Is that your truck?" I asked.

She nodded. I waited for her to say something, but she didn't.

"Are you a landscaper?" I asked.

"A gardener."

What the fuck? I stared at her. "Is there a difference?"

She didn't like me, thought I was a jerk. I didn't have to be psychic to know that. She pointed to a Hispanic work crew a few doors down. "If you need someone to mow, you might could ask them."

"So you don't mow?" Was she a snob? A gardening snob? Was there such a thing? The economy was pretty bad. Didn't she want the job?

"Sometimes I mow," she said.

I didn't get this chick at all. I wiped my sweaty face with my sleeveless arm and made a frustrated noise.

She took a step toward my car and pointed to the landscaping crew again. "Ask them. If you just need a mow and blow service, I'm sure they'll be happy—"

"Mow and blow?"

"I take care of plants. Occasionally I mow lawns, but I'm mainly a horticulturist. If you need your lawn cut—"

Did I need more than that? She was kind of cute. "Why don't you tell me what I need?"

She gave me a head tilt like she couldn't decide if I was rude or a pervert.

"I live down there." I pointed. "The house with the really long grass."

She looked down the street and nodded. "I'll come down after I finish."

"Great." I pointed to the liquor sack. "I've got refreshments."

I smiled, but didn't like the look she gave me. She felt sorry for me. I no longer confused kindness with pity. I drove off without saying goodbye and didn't care if she came by or not. A snooty gardener or landscaper or whatever the hell she was, I didn't need it.

The doorbell rang an hour later. She had a different attitude when I opened the door.

She smiled and held out her hand. "Nicole Westlake. I own Floratropolis. You wanted me to look around."

"Come inside. We'll walk through to the back."

"Nice place," she said, carefully wiping her feet on the doormat and then stepping inside.

"Thanks. I lived in a condo before. It didn't occur to me to worry about the lawn." My tongue felt heavy. I was slurring my words.

I led her from the foyer, through the hardwood hallway, and into the kitchen. "Want a drink?" I asked.

She glanced up at the clock. It was a little after two. "No, thanks." She was carrying a water bottle and took a swig from it. "I don't live far from here, but I don't have a lot of clients out in this area. I mostly work in Midtown and Buckhead."

I shrugged. I didn't know the area well. The names of neighborhoods meant little to me.

"How long have you lived here?" she asked.

"About a month. I guess I need someone to take care of the lawn."

She looked out the back window into the yard. "Great space. Do you use the pool?"

The pool was a whole other thing. It'd seemed like a good idea at the time, but now I had to find someone to take care of it, like the lawn.

"I haven't yet."

She opened the back door and went out. I followed.

"Wow, this is wonderful. I'm sorry—what's your name?"

I hadn't introduced myself. I was hammered and unfocused. "Kelleher Digby. Call me Kell." I licked my lips. I wasn't making a favorable impression. "I'm kind of going through a bad time."

She barely glanced at me as she sized up the back yard. "We've all been there, Kell."

Just the way she said it, I was ready to hand over my checkbook. She was all business, a real professional. She reminded me of the way I used to be, except she was a gardener and I was a killer.

"I don't know what your budget is, but I can help," she said. "I'll be back in a minute." Nicole went back inside. I tried to sober up. I was making a fool out of myself.

She returned with a sketchbook and pencil. I swatted at mosquitoes while she sketched.

"You can go in if you want. The bugs are awful. Next time I come out, I'll bring mosquito dunks." She motioned with her shoulder toward the pool. "You really should get the pool taken care of. I know someone good who can—"

"Yeah," I said, waving at her, "take care of it."

By the time she left, she'd sold me on a design for the front and back yards, called a pool person who agreed to come out the next day, and told me she lived with her partner who was named Nora. I think the last part came about because of something embarrassing I said or did. She didn't hold it against me. I imagined her saying, "She's a mess, Nora." About me.

Nicole started coming by once a week. The yard looked much better, and she even mowed. She kept telling me that I should get someone else because, one, she wasn't the best mower in the world, and, two, I was paying her seventy-five dollars an hour. I honestly didn't care as long as it got mowed. She sent me a bill. I paid it, mailing it in the envelope she'd sent with the bill.

I was still sleeping a lot. Sometimes the whole day. A month after I met Nicole, I was up in bed when I heard a commotion downstairs that brought me out of a dead sleep. I snatched the loaded gun out of the nightstand. Gun pointing, I walked to the door and listened. Slowly, things came into focus.

"Kell!" It was Nicole's voice. I rubbed my face, put away the gun, and yelled, "I'll be right down."

"Were you asleep?" she called up. "Sorry. I need to talk to you, but I'll come back."

"It's okay. I'll be down in a minute."

I looked at the clock. It was a little after three in the afternoon. She must think I'm a real loser, I thought to myself, as I hurriedly put on jeans and a shirt. I looked at myself in the mirror before I went down. Wow. I used to be such a pretty girl. Now I looked like Amy Winehouse after smoking crack for a week. *Wow.* I had major bedhead and Nesquik residue on both mouth corners. I wiped at the crud with my shirt sleeve.

Nicole was standing against the back door when I came down. "You were asleep," she said in a regretful voice. "I'm sorry. I didn't mean to disturb your nap."

She thought I was napping. What time had I gone to bed? A little after midnight. I'd slept and slept. It had to be the drugs because I still felt tired.

"It's okay. Really."

"The door was open," she said.

"I guess I forgot to lock it."

"No. I mean, the door was *open.* Wide open."

"Oh."

A piece of paper was in her hand. She held it up. It looked like a check.

"You made a mistake on the check," she said.

"Did I forget to sign it?"

"No." Nicole handed it to me. "You made it out for a million dollars." She laughed.

I stared at it, trying to comprehend. "It's covered."

She beamed and winked at me. "I'm sure it is, Miss Kell.

Nora's wondering exactly what I'm doing over here." She paused. "A bad breakup?"

"Something like that."

We shared a knowing smile.

"God, it's freezing in here," she said, rubbing her arms. "You like it cold."

"I'll write you another check. I'm sorry." Nicole put the original invoice in front of me. I focused as I wrote the new check. "Do you go out to the park much?"

"Stone Mountain? Sure. I take the dogs out there. They love it. Sometimes Nora and I climb the mountain or hike the trails. You should get a pass."

"Yeah. I had one, but I think it fell off." I handed her the check.

"You need to be careful. A guy got murdered out there a few months ago. On the trail. It was probably Mafia or something, but still it's kind of scary." She shivered, though it might have been from the air conditioning. "I don't like the idea of someone out there with a gun. I hate guns."

"So do I. Thanks for the heads up."

I didn't go to the park that day or the next. In fact, not much was different in my life over the next few weeks. I was in a rut. I fully expected to get out of it at some point, but the truth was that it probably would have happened later rather than sooner if it hadn't been for Rosa.

12

"Don't hang up."

"Why would I hang up, Rosa?"

"I'm in your driveway," she said. "Can I come in?"

It was late afternoon, and I'd been up for about an hour when the phone rang. I was in the middle of pouring Fruity Pebbles into a cereal bowl.

I don't usually answer my phone, but when I saw Rosa's name appear on the screen, I have to admit I was curious. I hurried to the window and slid my fingers through the slats.

The green Jag sat in the driveway. Rosa was in the driver's seat with a phone to her ear. Our eyes met.

I went to the front door, opened it, and stepped back. A car door shut. Footsteps came toward me. It was going to take a lot of nerve for Rosa to walk through the doorway. I put down the phone, folded my arms, and waited.

Rosa stepped inside. We stared at each other. I got the feeling she wanted to do the whole huggy thing. I wasn't in the mood.

She'd lost weight and wore a print dress that I didn't recognize. She was wearing light makeup. Her nails were done. Rosa was taking care of herself.

"How have you been?" she asked. "Your head looks so

much better. You can't even tell."

In fact, the scar was minor and mostly hidden by my hair. Still, I was self-conscious. I looked rough and knew it.

"What do you want?" I asked.

"I need a big favor."

"You must be out of your fucking mind. Why in the world would I do something for you?"

"I'll tell you about your sister."

I read her eyes. Was she bullshitting me? *My sister?* I had a sudden dreadful thought.

"*You?*"

Rosa rolled her eyes. "*No!* What is wrong with you? Do you really think I would have slept with you if I—you must think I'm the worst person who's ever lived."

Well, that got me going.

"I don't know, Rosa. You set me up. Tried to get me killed. Oh, first you gave me a little party, last meal in a sense, and then you and your girlfriend played me for a complete fool. Because you didn't need me anymore—and you didn't want to pay for my final job *and* you wanted my life insurance policy and portfolio." I took a breath. "You fucking tried to kill me."

"That's not how it was, Kell. That's not what I had in my head. You never gave me a chance to explain. You can believe what you want, but—"

I motioned for her to close the front door. She was reluctant, fearful that closing the door meant I was going to harm her. I might at that. I wasn't as tough as I used to be, but Rosa was a girly-girl. Even now, I could take her.

"Will you act civilized?" she asked.

"*Civilized?*" My face contorted with rage. "*Civilized?* Quit being a fucking baby and shut the fucking door!"

Rosa closed the door and leaned against it. When she began speaking again, her voice was lower, more measured. "I thought it was the best solution. I was responsible for you. I wanted out. I didn't know what would become of you. I'd been telling you that I wanted out."

"You never said that."

"I did." She pointed her finger at me. "You didn't listen. You didn't want to hear it. Every time I brought it up, you changed the subject."

I thought back. She'd made comments about doing something different. I hadn't taken them seriously.

"You started acting crazy," she said. "I was afraid you were going to tell people what you'd done. You kept wanting to date cops. Take risks. You were unprofessional."

That one stung. "I was like a pet that got old. You decided it was time to put me down."

She shook her head. "I didn't see how you could live in civilized society." Rosa looked me up and down. "I mean, look at you." She let it sink in.

"I was much more attractive before you sent me to Atlanta."

Now, not so much. I'd lost weight. I hadn't showered in a couple days. My hair was stringy and tangled. It hadn't been cut in months. I had on a stained undershirt and reindeer pajama bottoms. They weren't mine. I'd found them in a chest of drawers in one of the bedrooms.

"I'm sorry, Kell. I figured you'd start drinking. Become a drug addict. Something bad. You might make a mistake and go to prison. I was responsible for you. I thought it was the best choice. What I did, I did out of love. I told her to give you the best goddamn time of your life." Rosa started crying. "I agonized over it, but I couldn't imagine your life—well, I could imagine it. I couldn't bear it."

"I'm fine."

She shook her head, still weeping.

"I am. I'm alive."

Rosa covered her mouth. "I can't bear to look at you. Look at what you've become." Like me, Rosa isn't much of a crier, but when she unloads, she's messy. She pulled Kleenex out of her purse and wiped and blew. I felt sorry for her.

"God, Kell," she said, reaching out with her Kleenex and wiping at my eyes. "You've got eye goo all over your face."

I pulled back and scowled, groaning and moaning like a child in a department store dressing room. I picked at the eye boogers. "I don't know what you want or expect me to do," I said. "I won't be any good to you. Find someone else. I'm not in shape. I haven't been at a firing range for—"

Rosa made a face. "I don't want you to kill anyone," she said, surprised that I'd reached that conclusion. "I had to close the business fast. Not everyone was thrilled. I'm working a con as a form of payment for shutting Ironclad. If I don't do it, things could get unpleasant. I need you."

She needed me. Rosa knew how to soften me.

"A con?" I asked.

Rosa nodded.

"Why can't Valerie do it?"

Rosa looked me over. "We need your physical type. It's about your sister."

"Explain that."

Rosa sighed. "Don't freak out."

I've always had a fascination for cons, and I have to admit I was intrigued by the sister talk. I folded my arms.

"We have to fake your death," she said.

I gave her a look. "Yeah. Right." I laughed. This was the funniest damn thing I'd heard in a long time. "Don't count on it."

"Not *your* death but someone who looks like you."

"Aren't you going to a lot of trouble to finish me off?" I ran upstairs and grabbed the gun from the nightstand drawer.

"What are you doing?" Rosa called up nervously.

I hurried back down, carrying the Glock. When she saw it, she turned white and backed against the door. "Kell." Her hands went up to shield herself.

"Here," I said, holding it out to her with the barrel pointing at me. "Finish me off." I kept coming towards her. "Don't give me all this crap about a con where you might have to fake my fucking death. With a fucking sister who doesn't exist." I was a foot from Rosa, motioning her to take the gun.

Rosa stared at the gun. She made no attempt to take it. Neither of us said anything for a long time.

"You're scaring the fuck out of me with that thing," she finally said. "For God's sake, put it down. Please."

I set it on the coffee table. She let out one long, relieved breath.

"What you're telling me, it's for real?"

She nodded.

"How much?" I couldn't imagine ever running out of money, but I was curious.

"Twenty for you. Twenty for us." The "us" hurt. "The other party is getting the big payoff. I'm not sure what he's getting. It's his con. I facilitated it, but he's doing the tough stuff."

"Because you owe him." This was nickel and dime stuff for Rosa. She wasn't in it for the money.

"Yes."

"The sister thing—"

"She's not getting conned, but she's part of it." Rosa thought for a minute. "An innocent party in a sense. Her boyfriend is a big loser boy. Rich guy. Married. We're gonna convince him he killed his girlfriend. Your sister. We'll do a cleanup for him for a large sum of money. Get rid of the body. Cover up the death."

"How are you going to convince him she's dead?"

"That's where you come in. Are you in? If you are, I'll tell you about your sister."

Rosa knew how to play me. "Fine. I'm in."

13

"Before your parents got married, they had a baby," Rosa said. "They thought they were too young to take care of her, so they gave her to some friends."

"How do you know this?"

"Your mother confided in me. Your parents were cool, Kell. They gave the baby to some friends who moved to California. Your folks promised they wouldn't contact her. Your mom said she knew they'd done the right thing, but it bothered her some, you know, wondering and all."

"What's her name?"

"Virginia Moorehead."

"She doesn't know she's adopted."

"I don't know what she was told. She hasn't tried to contact you. If she knows, she hasn't gone out of her way to connect with you."

"I look like her."

"There's a resemblance."

"Why didn't you tell me before?"

"I didn't see any reason to. I promised your mother I'd never tell anyone."

"So how—"

"Like I said, a colleague wasn't happy about the business

closing," Rosa said. "I was planning on shutting down, but not right away. After you took the money, I had to close sooner than I planned."

"I didn't take all the money."

"You took a lot. It was a crazy time. There's a guy I'd hired to do some work. He was counting on a couple more jobs. I had to come up with something. I found out about your sister and her involvement with this guy. My colleague is already in California, palling around with the loser."

"How do you know she's seeing a married man?"

"There are people I keep tabs on. She's one of them. You never know when it might turn into something."

You had to admire Rosa's self-interest.

"What's she like?"

"I have her folder in the car."

I nodded. Rosa went outside to her car and returned with her briefcase. She brought out the folder and handed it to me. I took it to the couch, sat, paused a moment, and opened it.

"She looks kind of geeky," I said, after staring at a color 8x10 photo for several moments. It showed a woman several years older than me. She was thin and wore dark glasses. Her blonde shoulder-length hair was pulled back.

I looked for the similarities first. Oval-shaped faces. Our hair parted in the same place. Almost identical noses.

She was thinner than me. Or at least had been. We were about the same size now. Also, my eyes were larger. My mouth, smaller.

"She's a psychology professor," Rosa said. "*Dr.* Virginia Moorehead."

I looked up.

"At Oceanvue University," she said.

I stared at the photo. "There's no doubt."

"None."

"Do you think she looks like me?" I asked, holding up the

picture to my face.

"If we dye your hair, get you glasses and contacts, steal some of her clothing and get you into them, the resemblance will be uncanny."

"How tall is she?"

"You're taller, but it's not going to matter."

"She lives in California?"

"All her life."

"How much older is she?"

"Three years."

I couldn't help but think about how different her life must have been. Same genetics and a totally different path.

"Do you know anything about the people who raised her?" I asked.

"Professionals. Mom's a lawyer. Dad's a dentist. She has two brothers. They appear to be a good family. All the kids have Ph.D.s."

"You don't know if she was ever told—"

"She's adopted? I don't know. Will you be able to handle this, Kell? You'll have to stay focused."

"You can count on me," I lied. I doubted myself. I wasn't the person she'd sent to Atlanta months before. For one thing, I had to stop drinking. I had to stop the antidepressants. I was in a routine where I slept eighteen hours a day.

Rosa looked at me like she didn't believe me.

"Color my hair," I said, like I only now realized what she'd said. I looked at the photo again. "Do you think that's her natural color?"

Rosa shook her head. "No. Your parents both had brown hair. I imagine her natural color is like yours."

"What will I look like blonde?" I asked, touching a strand of my matted hair.

"Her."

"She has brown eyes."

"She didn't get your gray eyes, sweetie. We'll get you brown contacts."

"Tell me the con again. Wait. Let me take a shower. Will you brew some coffee?"

The coffee was ready when I came back downstairs. I dressed in my own clothes this time, even though they hung loosely on me.

Rosa had filled two mugs. She always drank he coffee black. She'd put sugar and half-and-half in mine. It felt like the old days. Rosa was all business when I sat down.

"You and I will drive to California," she said. "Richard Donnigan is already there. He's become Michael Rayburn's friend. Richard drinks with him. He's developed a rapport. We'll get your hair colored and cut so it matches hers. We'll get you eyeglasses and colored contacts. She goes to the dry cleaner once a week. She drops off her clothes on Friday and picks up on Monday. We'll borrow a few pieces of clothing. Take photos of you dressed like her. You'll look beaten and dead."

I gave her a look.

"Makeup, sweetie. Meanwhile, Richard goes out with Michael, slips a roofie into his drink. Michael passes out. He wakes up. Richard is in full drama mode." Rosa waved her hands. "'You've killed your girlfriend. Here are the photos. I'll get you out of this, but you have to pay me 'x' amount of money.' Michael may insist on calling her. He can't believe it. He'll call, but she won't answer. He may try her family, some friends. No one's seen her. No one can get in touch with her." She paused. "You've kidnapped her."

I put down my mug. "*I've* kidnapped her?"

"You've stopped wearing her glasses and clothes. Your hair is dyed back. She won't see a resemblance because she isn't looking for one." She took a sip. "She'll also be blindfolded and bound."

"I don't know, Rosa." I leaned back, took another sip, and put down the mug. "How am I going to kidnap her?"

"She teaches a night class. You break into her car and wait till her class ends. We have a place you can take her. It's a beach house that belongs to a friend of Richard's. When the deal's done, you let her go."

"How will I get her to go along with me?"

"With a gun."

"Get Valerie to do that part."

Rosa cocked her head and gave me a long look. "That's not her strength. Valerie is not part of this."

"You want me to point a gun at my sister who doesn't know she's my sister?"

"I'm not asking you to hurt her. She won't get hurt at all."

"She'll be scared to death. She's probably never had a gun pointed at her in her life. Don't you think?"

"Then she'll do what you ask. You'll spend time with her. Ask about her life. Get out all the questions without arousing suspicion. Then you're gone. She's safe. Hopefully she realizes the guy is a loser and leaves him. She has a great story to tell her kids someday." Rosa paused and drank her coffee. "You already told me you'd do it."

I had. That was true. I didn't mind working again. In fact, this was the best I'd felt in a long time. Still, I didn't know if I could act tough to this stranger who was actually my flesh and blood.

"She's going to be afraid," Rosa said. "What sane person is going to argue with a chick with a gun?"

"What if something goes wrong?"

Rosa tilted her head back and sighed. "In some ways, this is going to be one of the easiest jobs you've ever pulled. Would you be acting like this if you didn't know she was your sister?"

Of course not.

"You *need* to do this, Kell."

14

"You were right about the taxes," I said, after we'd been driving for a while. It hadn't taken me long to pack, and Rosa was eager to hit the road.

A couple of months after the Atlanta thing, Rosa had sent me a W-2 along with the tax form already filled out. She'd mailed it to my Chicago condo, but it was forwarded to me in Stone Mountain. The amount I owed the IRS was astronomical.

"I tried to tell you," she said.

"It almost made a Republican out of me. Are you two still together?"

She didn't miss a beat. "Yes. We're moving to Florida." Rosa glanced at me. "Thank you for not killing her."

"I wasn't hired to kill her."

"Most people would have. And killed me too."

I looked out the window.

"It wasn't what it looked like," she said.

"Rosa." I didn't want to rehash it. It was exactly what it looked like. Now Rosa was in trouble and needed me. She didn't want me to think I'd been punked.

"I'm telling you, sweetie, it wasn't."

"Okay."

"Did you have to put tape in her hair? It was a real mess, let me tell you."

I smiled at her. She smiled back and reached over, squeezing my hand. "Kell, Kell, Kell."

I didn't know what to say to that, so I remained quiet. In a moment, Rosa said, "She never felt right about killing you. She agreed to it, but she didn't like the idea."

"You should have hired a whore and a hit man. Seriously, Rosa. Yeah, let her soften me up, but get a real killer. Lure me to the cabin and pick me off before I even get to the door. This is what she did." I mimicked Valerie holding out a gun with two hands and firing with eyes closed.

Rosa shrugged. "I was trying to keep it small. Little baseball. It was a mistake. It was all a mistake. Mine. I honestly thought it was the best solution. That's why I want to get out of it. My decision-making isn't good anymore. I would have regretted it forever, Kell. So would she."

"What were you going to do with the body?"

Rosa didn't answer for a long time. "It's unpleasant." She glanced over at me and then back at the road.

"It wouldn't have been found, would it?" Rosa didn't answer. "Then how were you going to get the life insurance?"

"I told you it wasn't about that. Kell, if I wanted your money I could have taken it any time. I had 24-7 access to your money, sweetie."

"That's true," I admitted.

"In fact—" Rosa hesitated before completing her next sentence. "I *have* 24-7 access. Any time you change your password, the information gets sent to me in an email. The point is this, if it was about the money, I could have taken it whenever I wanted."

I thought about this a long time. "Hmm."

"I've been wanting to talk to you about your allocations. You've got a lot sitting in a money market. You really need to get those funds into equities. Especially with the market down. It's going to pop, and you're going to be sorry you were sitting on the sidelines."

I sighed.

"Do you want me to take care of it?" Rosa asked.

"Knock yourself out."

"Good. It's been driving me—"

"How'd you meet Valerie?"

"In Vegas."

I looked at her.

She nodded. "She was a working girl. I fell for her."

"When two people meet and fall in love, someone's got to die," I said. Another one of Rosa's sayings. "You were laughing at me."

She gave me a sharp look. "Absolutely not. Every conversation with her started with, 'I can't do this.' It was an awful time. Just terrible. We *never* laughed at you. Things were tense. There was nothing funny about it. I was a fucking nervous wreck, and so was she."

"You brought home a bottle of wine," I said in a monotone, intentionally trying to keep emotion out of my voice.

"I was freaking out, Kell. I hadn't heard from either of you in more than twelve hours. I couldn't get you or her on the phone. I couldn't stand it anymore. When you're stressed, you have sex or work out. "When I'm stressed, I—"

"Shop."

"The wine was to calm me down. I was *not* celebrating."

Perhaps not ironically, we stopped at a Trader Joe's so we could get snacks before we got out of Georgia. "You need to start eating better," Rosa said. "I assume you've been eating crap."

Kid cereal like Cocoa Puffs and Fruity Pebbles, along with white toast and Nesquik, were my regular menu items. I was less worried about eating better than I was about sleep. Rosa had banned alcohol and insisted that I stop taking anything to help me sleep. I was scared. I finally confessed my fears to Rosa when we stopped for the night at a hotel in Arkansas.

"You've got to get that stuff out of your system," she said. "It's not going to be easy. You're probably addicted to it. I'll sit up with you until you can sleep."

I had my doubts. Before we went to bed, Rosa briefly called Valerie. I figured she said something about me because, at one point, she glanced over, stared at me for a moment, and then said, "No. It'll be okay."

Rosa made me take a hot shower. "It should make you sleepy," she said. Although we had two beds, she climbed into the same bed with me and pulled me to her. She laid me down and put her hand on my chest. "I'll stay until you fall asleep."

"I don't think it's going to work." I was near panic. It was comforting to have Rosa touch me, but I was wide awake. "You thought I was irredeemable," I said.

"I was wrong."

Despite everything, I was thrilled to have Rosa fussing over me again. I didn't want to feel that way, but I did. At the same time, neither of us seemed to be feeling anything sexual. I figured that was over. I also figured she and Valerie were exclusive. Whatever.

"Sh-sh-sh-sh," Rosa said, stroking my face and chest with her hand.

It didn't work. She massaged my back, my feet, my head. I don't know how much sleep she got that first night, but I only slept two or three hours total. Each night got better.

In Austin, we had my hair cut and dyed. She also got me dark-rimmed glasses and colored contacts at a Visionworks in a mall. She insisted that I take the eye test.

"When's the last time you had your eyes checked?" she asked.

I couldn't remember, so she made me do it. Turns out, I'd lost some distance and close-up vision. Not much, but enough to need prescription lenses for distance. The doctor said I didn't need bifocals—thank God—but suggested I pick up reading glasses from the drugstore.

"I'm not going to wear them after this," I told Rosa while we ate at an Italian restaurant in the same mall.

"I don't think they look bad," she said, scrutinizing me. I was wearing eyeglasses that were like my sister's. "It gives you a scholarly look. More serious. I like it. It's hot, sweetie."

"Do I look like her yet?"

She eyed me. "You're getting there. You're better looking though."

"Maybe it's because I have an edge to me."

"Maybe. You've got prettier eyes." Rosa winked at me.

I laughed and ate more bread.

Rosa looked down at her ravioli. "She would have been a better influence on you. There's no telling how things might have turned out."

"Rosa."

She looked at me. I shook my head and waved my hands. It was done. She nodded.

15

Richard Donnigan was one scary dude. No wonder Rosa was afraid of him. I was afraid of him. You'd be a damn fool not to fear this man. He was well over six feet tall and easily weighed 250. He might have been part Native American or Italian or something. He had black hair, slicked back with some kind of gel. Danger emanated from him like heat from a toaster. When he smiled, his lips twitched, and his mouth didn't open.

I shook his hand. Of course, he insisted on hugging. Ugggghhhhh. Rosa, standing behind him, gave me a look, willing me not to shudder. I'm a pro. I didn't.

"I've heard a lot about you," he said, smiling, checking me out. He kept touching me and pretty much did everything but put his hand down my pants.

I shot a glance at Rosa. Her mouth was tight, and her arms were folded. Richard put his arm around me and hugged me closer to him. Rosa looked like she was glad it was me and not her.

"This is going to be fun," he said. He rubbed his hands together, but then realized they weren't on me and started fondling me again.

"Whoa, cowboy," I said, backing off. Enough was enough. He put up his hands to say he'd meant no harm, but then became

Mr. Grabby again.

"Tell me about yourself, Richard," I said, weaving away from him.

"I'm a professional," he said. "Pretty much done it all. Need a little more moolah before I can chill. I'm from Vegas. That's where I met Rosa."

I cut a glance at her. She grimly nodded.

"How did you meet that clown?" I asked later, when Rosa and I were alone in our cheap motel room. We weren't staying here but had rented it for the day. We were staying at a really classy place with a view of the ocean.

I hate motels like this. Everything was inexpensive and fake. We were here because, according to Rosa, this was the kind of place where Michael and Virginia met to have sex. I was beginning to hate this guy. He's rich, and he can't spring for a classier place to fuck her?

"You meet a lot of interesting people in my business," Rosa said.

"He doesn't seem bright enough to do this."

"Don't underestimate him. It'll be fine. He's a pro."

"I don't think he's cool."

"He's cool."

"Hasn't he pretty much extorted you into doing this?"

"I wouldn't put it like that." Rosa didn't want to discuss it. "You should be relieved he's not doing the kidnapping. You want him around your sister?"

"He's been in prison, hasn't he?"

"How can you tell?"

"I can tell." There was a metal-like hardness to people who'd been in prison. Maybe they had it before they went in, but I personally think they developed it there. "You don't like to deal with ex-cons."

"I don't have a choice." Rosa gave me a meaningful look.

"What if he fucks up?"

"If you want to know the truth," she said, "I've actually got more faith in him than you on this one. If anyone's going to fuck up, it'll be you."

"Gee, thanks."

"Just being honest. His head is clear."

"I'm not going to let you down."

"I know you won't." Rosa wanted me to shut up. "Look, Kell. We can't fuck this up. Richard is not the type of guy—" She gave me a hard look. "It's imperative this go well, or we'll never be seen again. There's no other way for me to put it."

She let it sink in.

"What's going on in Vegas?" I asked. "I didn't know you did business there."

"Kell, there are lots of things you don't know. Obviously."

"Was Hank Kingsley a Vegas connection?"

Rosa nodded.

"Some of that money I took—it was Vegas money, wasn't it?"

"It certainly was, sweetie."

"I put you in a bad position."

Rosa laughed and tilted her head. "It was a pickle. Piece of cake, it *wasn't*. We both played hardball. You won."

"Rosa, I'm sure you can see it's difficult to trust you."

"I can see that."

I kept wanting her to say something else. She stared back at me.

"Maybe this whole thing is another con," I said. "You playing me again."

"No."

She took my face in her hand and gently kissed me. Then kept kissing me. I had a lot on my mind, or I would have reacted more. Still, it was surprisingly hot.

"That makes me think it even more," I said.

"I'm not."

"What would you say to me if you *were* conning me?"

"Kell, I know you don't trust me right now. I promise on your parents' graves that I've told you the truth about this. I didn't tell you about the Vegas thing because, frankly, it didn't concern you." Rosa took my hands. "Really, sweetie."

I didn't have a choice. Things were going quickly now. There was no turning back.

Virginia's stolen outfit consisted of a pair of unflattering black pinstripe trousers and a lightweight green cotton sweater. Rosa also handed me a yin-yang necklace. Apparently Virginia wore something like this all the time. The necklace was black leather, and the symbol was silver and rosewood. Finally, Rosa gave me a black Timex watch to put on my wrist.

I put in the brown contacts and put on the eyeglasses. I looked in the mirror and saw Miss Frumpy Frump from Frumpsville.

Rosa dumped out a bag of movie makeup onto the shiny, cheap-looking credenza in front of a window that looked out onto a dumpster. "Close enough," she said, looking at my reflection. "We're selling the idea more than anything."

Richard showed up a few minutes later with a camera. Obviously we were using a Polaroid camera because we couldn't take pictures of a 'dead' woman up to CVS.

Rosa applied the makeup while Richard supervised. By the time they were done, I looked like I'd had the shit beaten out of me. They posed me on the hotel bed for a few dozen photos.

Rosa and I horsed around and got the giggles a few times. In truth, it was the most fun I'd had in a long time. I was grateful to Rosa for getting me out of my rut. Even if our plan resulted in my death, at least I was finally doing something productive again.

Richard took photos of us goofing. Rosa thought I looked like a vampire, so I pretended to bite her neck while she mugged for the camera. Things like that.

Rosa sternly warned Richard though. "No memorabilia, bub," she said. "You know what needs to be done with these. I don't want to see any of this on an evidence table. Everything destroyed afterward. Got me?"

Richard hung his head and had that sick grin on his face. "Yes. Got you. You two should be on a reality TV show. I know the logistics would be tough, but, wow, who wouldn't watch that?" His eyes lit up. "I could make guest appearances. I know a producer who owes me a favor. Maybe I can pitch it."

"Leave our names out of it," Rosa said.

"That goes without saying. You need aliases. I was thinking we'd have to blot out your faces, but you're both too pretty for that. Let me think about it. There's got to be a way around it." Richard was wincing because he was thinking hard. Again, I had serious doubts that he could pull off anything.

Richard finally announced that we had enough shots. He lined up the photos on the credenza. We silently observed each one. I thought they were pretty damn good.

I compared the photos with the one of Dr. Moorehead. Death can change features, but the photos were convincing. Plus, I was wearing her clothing and replicas of her jewelry. It was genius. The loser boyfriend would believe he'd killed his girlfriend.

Rosa glanced down at the photos and scooped up the ones that featured the two of us.

"Oh, come on," Richard whined.

Rosa ignored him.

"Just a couple," he pleaded. "I'll pay you for them," he said.

Rosa handed them to me.

Richard was pouty. I started to worry. Rosa must have had second thoughts too. She softened and snatched the photos from me. "You can pick *one*," she told a gleeful Richard. It took him a long time, but he finally chose one that was the most lesbian. We weren't really kissing, but it looked like we were.

"I don't want to see that up on eBay," I said.

Finally, it was time for Richard to do his thing. Meanwhile, I got out of the clothes and contacts and went with Rosa to a hair salon. In a few hours, I was back to my natural brown. I was still wearing the glasses and necklace. I fingered the necklace while riding back to the luxury hotel with Rosa. "Maybe it'll bring good luck," I said.

"I don't believe in luck, sweetie. I believe in not fucking up. Are you okay?"

"I'm okay."

16

"What if she opens the back door of her car to put in a backpack or something?" I asked. "Did you consider that?"

I'd gone over the scenario with Rosa several times and was studying a photo of Virginia's four door Volvo sedan.

"She always carries a briefcase," Rosa said. "Every time we've watched her, she's opened her door and tossed it on the passenger seat."

"What if she doesn't this time?"

Rosa stared at me. I didn't back down.

"Scrunch up on the floor, so she doesn't see you." Rosa paused. "Or you could finger your necklace and pray."

I didn't appreciate the sarcasm.

"Make it absolutely clear that you'll hurt her, but if she does everything you say, she'll be fine. It's up to you about what you'll do if she runs. You know what's at stake."

I swallowed. "How do I get the blindfold and rope on her?" I was acting like a baby, like I didn't know how to do anything.

"We've gone over the route. Take her to the road in front of the abandoned plant. Make her get out of the car, slip the blindfold over her head, and bind her hands. Put her back in the car, in the passenger seat, and take her to the beach house."

"What if her boyfriend won't agree to Richard's demands?"

Rosa didn't say anything for a while. "If things fall apart on his end," she finally said, "I'll get word to you. You'll drop her off somewhere. You and I will meet up and get the hell out." She leaned over and squeezed my hand. "I know you're scared, Kell. We'll get through this one way or another. We always have." This was true. Something else was true. If people do bad things enough times, they'll eventually get caught. Maybe it was our turn.

"You're on board with the ski mask, right?" Rosa asked.

We'd argued about this. I didn't want to wear it. I can't stand anything covering my face. Rosa insisted.

"You got a clean one?" I asked.

Rosa handed me a shopping bag. "It's new. You need to do this just in case, Kell. If she were to see your face—"

"I'll wear it."

I opened the bag. "God, Rosa, it's ugly." She'd gotten me a buffalo plaid mask with a narrow slit for my eyes.

"They were all out of the pretty ones."

Virginia taught her night class on a campus housed in an office park. It didn't have an ocean or much of a view. According to Rosa, the main campus was a former seminary that offered a beautiful ocean view and looked like a traditional university with ivy-covered stone buildings and lush landscaping. This satellite campus, however, was charmless. The good news was that there wasn't much security. The parking lot had no gates, video cameras, or cops. When are people going to learn that the world isn't safe?

Rosa dropped me off after we drove by Virginia's car. I doubled back and had little trouble breaking into the Volvo with a master key. I crouched on the floor behind the passenger seat and put on the ski mask. If she opened a back door, it'd likely be the door behind the driver's seat. Hopefully, it'd be too dark for her to see me.

It was 9:45. Her class ended at 10. I waited and rubbed the necklace. Although I didn't know her, I figured that she was the type to hold the class the entire time. I also figured that there'd be some ass kissers who stayed after class. I might be here a while.

I heard people walking on the asphalt. Car doors slammed. Engines started. I was strangely calm. It wouldn't have done any good to worry. Things happen or don't happen. Worrying didn't change anything. I felt the way I had when I walked up to Valerie's cabin: I was in a movie.

The door locks clicked. Okay, now I was worried. Could I do this? Maybe I'd chicken out and ride along until we got to wherever she was going and then sneak away. Then what? Richard wasn't the kind of guy who'd put up with nonsense. I didn't want to experience his rage. Or Rosa's disappointment.

The car door opened. Something landed on the passenger seat. Virginia slid into the driver seat. The car door shut. The seatbelt clicked. The car started. Virginia must have been in a hurry because this all happened quickly.

I waited till she'd driven a few blocks. Just as she turned on the radio, I sat up. She must have caught my movement in her rear view mirror because she turned her head, alarmed. I was wearing the mask, but I instinctively held my hand over my face.

"Face the road," I said in a muffled voice. The car jerked a bit when I spoke, like she'd taken her foot off the gas pedal.

"Face forward," I said. "I have a gun. If you do what I say, you won't get hurt." I touched her shoulder with the gun so she wouldn't think I was bluffing.

"Keep driving," I said.

"What do you want?" She sounded scared but also irritated. It was the first time I'd heard her voice. What struck me was how much she sounded like Mom.

"I have a gun. I don't want to hurt you. Please do what I say. Don't look in the mirror, and don't turn around."

"Do you want the car?"

"No." I wasn't myself. Normally, I would have snarled, "No! I don't want the fucking car!" I heard myself sigh. I sounded like an amateur. "Take a right at the next street." I waited till the car was near the corner. "Now."

She did what she was told. If she'd ever imagined something like this happening, she probably hadn't imagined a woman barking orders. I wondered if she'd rehearsed what she'd do. It might occur to her to run, thinking that no matter what happened, it'd be far better than if she stayed with me.

We were on Hudson, a dark street with few street lights. An old, deserted towel factory was on the left side of the road. "Pull over now, stop the car, and shut off the engine," I said.

She followed my instructions. "Unlock my door," I said. She did. I quickly opened my car door but didn't get out. I grabbed hold of the back of her shirt and spoke close to her ear. "Get out of the car. Keep your back to me. Put your hands behind your back and clasp them."

She again obeyed. I got out and slipped a blindfold over her head. It was the kind that blocks out light for people trying to sleep. Rosa and I had gone back and forth on whether to get a sex or sleep blindfold. We concluded that the sleep one would do the same job but be more comfortable.

I clamped on Smith & Wesson handcuffs. The real thing—heavy and solid. Virginia trembled but didn't make a sound. I led her to the passenger side and opened the door. I grabbed her briefcase and said, "Watch your head." I guided her into the seat and ran back to the driver's side. Before I got in, I rifled through her briefcase, found her phone, turned it off, and tossed it and the briefcase in the back seat.

So far so good. We were ready to go. I started the car. The radio was still on. A PBS station was playing classical music. I turned it off. I put on my seatbelt and realized hers wasn't on. The alarm would irritate the fuck out of me, so I took off my seatbelt and leaned over to grab hers. She gasped and tensed.

"Relax. I'm putting on your seatbelt," I said.

She didn't relax, but I clicked it, put on mine, and drove away. I felt bad about the whole thing. I wanted to make a joke about whether she felt safer with her seatbelt on, but didn't think she'd find it amusing.

"It's going to be okay," I said, listening to her uneven breathing. "You'll be fine. You're not going to get hurt if you do what I say."

"Why are you doing this?" She sounded pissed off. I got the feeling that she wasn't used to being bossed around.

"It's not about you. We need to make someone think you're missing. Then we'll let you go."

I glanced at her. She was trying to figure it out. She faced me. The mask was on, and I knew she couldn't see me through the blindfold, but her looking right at me made me feel funny. "Don't look at me," I said.

She turned and faced forward. "Who? Who do you need—"

"I'll tell you later. I need to concentrate."

In one motion, I ripped off the itchy ski mask and stuffed it in my hoodie pocket. I glanced at Virginia. She was thinking, processing, trying to make sense of something that made no sense.

We arrived at the small beach house. The area was so isolated, I'd seen only two cars in the last ten minutes on the two-lane road.

I pulled into the gravel driveway and then gently onto the sandy grass in the back of the house. I got Virginia out of the car and led her inside through the back door.

I sat her down on a worn plaid sofa in the main room and went around turning on lights.

"Where are we?" she asked.

"I can't tell you that."

"Are you going to keep me blindfolded?"

"Yes."

"I thought it was just so I wouldn't know where we were going," she said in a panicky voice. She didn't want the blindfold on. A hard ocean wave crashed outside. She reacted by turning her head to the sound.

"Not entirely."

"Will you keep me handcuffed too?"

"Yep."

The house was dank, wet, and musty. I didn't like it at all. I don't like anything rustic. This place had knotty wood pine walls, pine furniture, and terrible nautical paintings on the walls. I was afraid to see the bathroom.

I sat on a round braided rug in front of the empty flagstone fireplace. She sat stiffly on the sofa, almost on its edge. I scrutinized her. So this was my sister.

"Are you still there?" she asked.

"Yes."

"What are you doing?"

"Sitting on the floor." I didn't tell her that I was staring at her. She knew.

"How long are we staying here?"

"I don't know. I honestly don't know."

"I have a class tomorrow at ten in the morning."

"You might not show up for it."

This alarmed her. "I've never missed a class in my life. People will start looking for me. They may start looking for me tonight."

"Who will look for you tonight?"

She clammed up.

"Your boyfriend?"

She wanted to say something but hesitated. I noticed her teeth were a lot like Dad's. The same shape. Good teeth. Straight and strong. I wondered if her smile was like his. I didn't figure she'd give me one.

"We know about the boyfriend," I said.

She took in a slow breath. "Is that what this is about?"

I didn't answer.

"Are you still there?" she asked.

"Yes. Did you know he was married?"

"God." She tossed her head back. Her face and neck flushed. I wondered if she was embarrassed or angry. Probably both.

"God" she said again. "His wife is doing this?"

"Not exactly."

"Are you her?"

This took me aback. "No. I'm not his wife. Did you know he was married?"

She didn't answer.

"It's your life," I said. "I certainly don't have any business giving advice. Tell me about yourself." I only had so much time. I needed to start asking questions.

"Is she going to hurt me?"

"The wife? No."

She remained quiet. I decided to goad her.

"I've heard he's a big loser," I said. "Why would you get involved with someone like that?"

"What's going to happen? You said you want it to look like I'm gone. Why?"

"Your boyfriend's getting set up. He's out hooting it up. You know how he is. Pretty soon he'll be convinced he's accidentally killed you."

"Why?"

"Money, honey."

"You think you'll get money from him because he thinks I'm dead?"

"Not only that you're dead, but he's responsible."

She took this in. "What if he doesn't pay?"

"He'll pay." I didn't tell her that there were photos. "Tell me about your life. What are your parents like?"

"Tell me about yours."

"You go first."

"They'll be worried. I call my mother first thing in the morning. If I don't call, she'll worry."

"What do you talk about?"

"How she is. She's been sick. She had breast cancer surgery a month ago. I check on her every morning. I tell her what I'm doing that day. The usual things you say to your mother. What do you say to your mother when you talk to her?"

I didn't answer.

"Will you tell her what you did tonight?" she asked.

I couldn't read her. Maybe she was trying to make me feel guilty. Maybe she was curious. I stood and stared out the window in the direction of the ocean, thinking how strange this conversation was. I also wondered what I'd be doing tonight if Virginia hadn't been given up for adoption, if my parents hadn't died. Maybe we'd be bowling or something.

"Do you bowl?" I asked.

"No."

"Neither do I."

She became quiet, probably thinking she was dealing with a lunatic.

"Do you get along with your brothers?" I asked.

"Why are you so interested in my family?" She was defensive. Her hands went into fists and then relaxed.

"You have two brothers. Very accomplished. I'm just curious. We've got to pass the time."

"You talk. I'll listen." She leaned back.

"You remind me of someone. Someone I used to know."

"Tell me about her."

Ah, she was using her psychology training.

"You're a psychologist, right?" I asked.

"I have a degree in psychology. I teach psychology. I'm not

technically a psychologist."

I wasn't interested in the distinction. "Do you like it?"

"Sure. Do you like doing this?"

There was a touch of contempt in her voice. It bothered me. "What is *this*?"

"I assume you're some kind of criminal."

"I'm a hit man."

17

"Or was," I said. "I don't know what I am now."

Virginia's mouth had opened slightly. I felt like a jerk for making her think I was going to kill her.

"Been to prison?" Her voice was unsteady.

"Never been arrested."

"You sound young."

She was trying to get as much information as she could, so she could tell the authorities later. "Here's something you don't understand," I said. "When all this is done, you can't go to the police." I let it sink in.

"Why's that?"

"Your boyfriend won't let you."

She gave a short laugh. "You think he has more control over me than he does."

"He's not going to let you because everything will come out. The affair, the con, everything. He'll want to put everything behind him. He'll want to put you behind him too."

She thought about this.

"This is going to be expensive for him," I said. "He'll blame you. Do you get along with your brothers?"

She leaned forward. "Have they been kidnapped too?"

"No," I assured her. "Just you. They're safe."

"But you know about them."

"Believe me. They're safe. I'm just curious about whether you get along with your siblings."

"Sure. Don't you get along with your siblings?"

I wanted to say not at the moment. In fact, I wanted to toy with her. It was stupid and dangerous. She had a fucking Ph.D. I needed to be careful.

"Do you have a favorite sibling?" I asked.

"I'm not comfortable talking about my family with you. I'm sorry. I don't want to anger you, but you've got me blindfolded and tied up. I'm scared. I don't know what you're going to do. The last thing I want to do is give you information about my family that you can use against them. Against us."

Us. She didn't realize we were 'us' too. "You're protecting them," I said.

"Yes."

"Fair enough. I admire you for it. I really do. Loyalty is a great character trait."

I was quiet for a long time. She settled back into the sofa again, sighing.

"Are you in love with your boyfriend?" I asked.

She shook her head. "I don't think so. I don't know."

"He's not good enough for you. At least from what I've heard."

She laughed and shook her head. "This is unreal."

"Is this one of those smart women, foolish choices things?"

"I guess. You've never made a mistake in a relationship?"

I laughed. "You have no idea," I said, still laughing. "By the way, I'm gay. You can imagine what goes along with that."

She didn't say anything, but, truly, what could she say?

"My childhood was pretty good up until I was sixteen," I said after a while.

"What happened?"

I ignored the question. "Did you have a good childhood?"

"Great," she said tersely.

"Good." I meant it.

"Tell me about yours." She didn't want to hear about my life. She wanted details, so she could nail me later. She still thought she'd be able to talk to the cops.

"Mom liked to bake. She made cakes, cookies, things like that. Dad liked to cook. He cooked almost all our meals. It was good stuff too. Macaroni and cheese. Pizza. Hot dogs and hamburgers. He'd put vegetables in casseroles, so they'd be easier to take. I think they had a good marriage. He had a temper. Like me. He wasn't violent or anything. He'd just go off, you know, yelling. He'd apologize later. Mom was laidback, easygoing. I wish I was more like her."

I was trying to give Virginia information about her birth parents. She should know about them. She was listening. "They were artsy people," I said. "Creative. They didn't like me watching TV. They wanted me to read. Books were important in the house. Music. Art. They let me do pretty much what I wanted."

"That's obvious."

I laughed. The funny thing was that she didn't realize how fucking hilarious this was.

"It's complicated," I said. "You and me. This situation. That's why I'm laughing. At least I'm not dating a loser." I wanted her to know that I was displeased with her relationship.

She reddened. "It's none of your business." Realizing she might have gone too far, she turned her head toward the window.

I wanted her attention again. "I got shot in the head."

She turned back to me. "That must have been quite an experience."

"It wasn't the worst thing that's ever happened to me."

"Do you want me to feel sorry for you?"

I wanted her to feel the connection between us. I wanted her to know she was my older sister, that we had the same parents. She sighed impatiently.

"Are you hungry?" I asked.

"No."

"Thirsty?"

"No. I just want to go home."

"Soon. Did you always like school? You've got a Ph.D. That takes a long time."

She nodded. "You seem to know a lot about me. Tell me more about this. Is Mike in danger?"

"He's getting played. If he's a good boy, he'll be fine. We've got to keep you here until the con is finished."

"Who's we?" She knew I wouldn't answer.

"If you want to sleep—"

"I can't sleep," she said wearily.

"How long have you been seeing this guy? Do you know his wife?"

"No."

"Do you feel guilty?"

"Do you feel guilty holding me against my will?"

"It's got to be done. Have you ever held a gun before?"

"No."

I'd used Rosa's computer to research Virginia. She was an expert on criminals. Women criminals, to be more precise. She'd done interviews with women prisoners and wrote papers on her research.

"So you study these criminals—" My telephone rang. "Hello," I said before it had a chance to ring twice.

"Everything okay?" Rosa asked.

"So far."

"Good," Rosa said. "Everything's going according to plan. He's convinced she's dead." She paused. "She's all right, isn't she?"

"Tip top."

"Good. He's getting the money. It should be done in an

hour or so. Are you okay?"

"Absolutely."

"I'll be in touch."

"What's going on?" Virginia asked when I closed the phone.

"With any luck, you'll be out of here soon."

She blew air out of her mouth. "Nothing like this has ever happened to me," she said almost giddily. "I guess I've lived a pretty boring life."

"I hate being bored."

"I do too, but I don't need this much excitement."

With the news that she might soon be released, Virginia's personality started coming out. We only had an hour or so left. I needed to find out what I could.

I was thinking about what I could ask when car lights outside the window caught my attention. Virginia didn't react. I stepped to the window and looked out. A police car passed by on the street. Fuck. I was glad my car was parked in the back. The car kept going.

"Will it change you?" I asked.

"It's certainly going to change my relationship with Mike."

I remained at the window. It was a good thing too. The car came back the other way and slowed.

"I'll be right back." I was out the door before she spoke. I stood on the porch until the cop parked his car on the side of the road and got out. I calmly strolled off the porch and walked toward his vehicle before he had a chance to shut his door. It was important she not hear our voices. If she figured out it was a cop, she might make a ruckus. I wouldn't have any choice but to kill the cop. Then I'd be in real trouble.

"Hey, man, how's it going?" I asked in my best California mellow accent.

"Evening, ma'am." He was smiling, wasn't nervous. "Everything all right with you tonight?"

"Pretty good. How about you?" He was young, crew-cut,

and muscular. The guy was like a puppy. I hoped I wouldn't have to use my gun. It was in the same pocket as the mask. I felt it and brought my empty hand back out.

"Beautiful night," he said and gazed up at the stars. He had a holstered gun and a night stick. He put two thumbs in the belt, relaxing.

We stood quietly for a few moments. "My boyfriend's asleep in there," I said, motioning with my shoulder toward the house. "We kind of had a fight." I moved my body toward his.

"Is that right?"

I glanced back at the house. "He can be a dick."

"I'm sorry to hear that."

I took a couple steps away from the house. He followed.

"So he's asleep, huh?" he asked.

"Yeah, but he's a light sleeper. I better get back in there."

"You sure?"

He took a pack of cigarettes out of his shirt pocket, lit a cigarette, and offered me one. I took it. "He's got a temper," I said. The cop lit the cigarette for me. I drew in hard. "He's leaving tomorrow night."

"Is that right?"

I glanced back at the house and quickly turned back to him. I kissed him on his lips. "Why don't you stop by later this week?" I asked. "Will you be on this route?"

"I can be," he said with a smile.

"That's great news."

I flashed a big smile back at him, leaned in, and gave him a real kiss. He started to embrace me, but I pulled away.

"I better go back," I said.

He moaned, winced, and implored me with his eyes. "Why don't you take a ride with me?"

"Because we'll both get in trouble, dude." I gently pushed him toward his car. "Come back in two nights."

107

18

The cop drove away, and I walked up to the house, finished the cigarette, and went back inside. Virginia sat erect, staring at the door.

"You're back." She sniffed. "You went out for a smoke?"

"Yeah. One of my many bad habits."

"I thought I heard you talking to someone. Was someone out there?"

I didn't answer her question. "What was the biggest turning point in your life?" I asked. "Besides this."

She thought for a moment. "Recently it's my mom's cancer."

She didn't say being adopted. She must not know.

"Everything's been pretty easy in my life up until then," she said. "My mother is—" She choked up. "I'm not afraid of dying. I don't want to be frightened or terrified or anything like that, but I'm not afraid of death. I'm afraid of other people's deaths."

"Yeah. Grief can do a real number on you."

She made a funny sound. She was crying but trying to stop. Shaking, she lowered her chin. "I'm sorry," she squeaked, before releasing horrendous sobs. She rocked back and forth on the sofa.

"Go ahead and cry. Sometimes it helps."

She rolled onto her side and shoved her face into the cushion. I shuddered, thinking how nasty the sofa's fabric was.

I figured I should do something, so I sat next to her and held my hand over the back of her head, afraid to touch her. After a moment, I rested my fingertips on her head. She pulled away and went into the fetal position. I rubbed her back. It felt warm and damp through her sweater.

She moved her head, so I could hear her plainly. "Please don't touch me."

I suspected she wanted to use stronger language but feared me. As it was, my feelings were hurt.

"I'm sorry your mother's sick," I said.

She drew further away from me.

"My mother died when I was young," I said, immediately wishing I hadn't. It was stupid to give her too much information. "I'm sorry," I said again. I meant I was sorry that I'd said anything, but she misunderstood.

She sat up, sniffling. "It's all right. It'll be fine."

"I'll find some tissue." The bathroom was as awful as I imagined it. I grabbed a handful of toilet paper and got out of there as fast as I could. I held the wad in my hand and realized she couldn't blow her nose. I made a decision.

"I'm going to unlock your cuffs, so you can blow your nose. Please don't try anything."

"I won't."

I got the key out of my jeans pocket and unlocked the cuffs. She rubbed the red marks on her wrists until she realized the tissue was in her lap. I moved off the couch. She blew several times and wiped her face. Her mouth quivered.

"Thank you," she said. "Would it be okay if I use the bathroom?"

"It's disgusting. I'm sorry, but it is."

She sighed and leaned back, defeated. Her hand clutched the tissue. "I should have peed before I left school. I thought I was going right home."

"It shouldn't be much longer."

"I'm blindfolded. How bad is the bathroom?"

"It's like the kind at truck stops."

"It doesn't sound that bad."

"I'm big on pristine bathrooms."

"In a perfect world, maybe, but I can't be picky right now."

"Have you ever camped?" I asked.

"Yes."

"It's like a bathroom at a campsite."

"Like I said, it doesn't sound that bad." She laughed. "You sound like you're used to the better things in life."

"I'm used to clean bathrooms. I never liked camping. My parents took me camping a few times when I was a kid. They loved it, but I hated every dirty, smelly, nasty minute. I see no reason to rough it if you don't have to. I'm all for enjoying nature. Do it for a few hours and then return to civilization. And clean bathrooms.

"I've camped a lot. I camped in China when I was younger. Rural China. The public restrooms were a hole in the ground." She stood. "I'm going for it. Can you lead me to the bathroom?"

Truthfully, I wasn't comfortable going into the bathroom with her, pulling down her pants, and waiting for her to finish. There were no windows, so I figured it'd be okay.

"All right," I said. "I'll lead you to the bathroom. Make sure the blindfold is on when you come out. Please don't do anything stupid."

"I just want to pee."

I took her by the wrist, led her to the bathroom door, and guided her in. I closed the door, leaned against it, and waited. Finally, I heard, "I'm ready."

"Is the blindfold on?"

"Yes."

She came out. "Thanks," she said. I led her back to the

couch. "It didn't seem that bad." Her mouth bent into a slight, almost teasing smile.

"I'll hold it. I need to cuff you again."

"Please don't." Virginia rubbed her wrists. "I won't try to get away. I promise."

"Do they hurt?"

"They're uncomfortable."

I thought for a long time.

"I'd really appreciate it," she said.

I sighed loudly, letting her know I wasn't pleased. "All right. But don't try anything."

"Promise."

"Do you worry about getting breast cancer now that your mom has had it?" I was still trying to figure out if she knew she was adopted.

"It's crossed my mind. Did your mom die of an illness?"

"No." I wanted to tell her everything.

"Did someone hurt her?"

"It was an accident. My father died too."

"I'm sorry."

Disgusted with myself, I walked away but turned back to face her when I reached the fireplace. "I'm lying to you. None of that happened."

She sat quietly and licked her lips.

"There are so many things I'd like to tell you. Know that," I said.

"What do you mean? "Tell me." Her voice was gentle, soothing.

"It would blow your mind."

She misunderstood. "I've heard just about everything. *This* surprised me, but I don't think there's anything that you could say that would shock me."

"You're wrong."

"If you think it would make you feel better—"

"I don't think it would make me feel better." I wanted to scream that we were connected. The impulse was almost too much. I went to the door, opened it, and looked out at the dark waves.

"Are you leaving?" she asked.

"No. Just getting some air."

"I've done counseling in the past. If you want to talk—"

"You don't understand." I turned and faced her. Again, I felt a horrible compulsion to tell her that she was my sister. I closed the door and walked back to the couch. When I sat, she didn't flinch. The blindfold seemed secure, but she turned to face me, so we were eye to eye.

"I want to understand," she said. Virginia reminded me of Mom. Her voice was similar as was her gentleness. In other ways, she was like Dad. She had his intensity, his good humor, and raw intelligence.

My phone rang. We both reacted with little jumps.

"Yeah," I said into the phone.

"It's done, sweetie," Rosa said. "Bring her back and let's get the hell out of here. You okay?"

"Came at a good time. I almost told her."

"Pull yourself together. It's almost over."

I felt dizzy.

"Don't make a mistake, sweetie," Rosa said. "We're so close. I know this is tough." She thought she was losing me. Her tone was sharp: Don't screw up, baby girl, or we'll all be in some deep shit.

"You're right," I said.

Rosa told me where to meet her.

I closed the phone. "Let's go. I need to cuff you again."

"Are you letting me go?" Virginia didn't believe it.

"Everything I promised."

She stood.

"Turn around and clasp your hands together," I said.

She did as she was told. I cuffed her and then embraced her, hugging her hard. "Have a good life," I said in her ear and let her go.

I'd done it fast, so she didn't have a chance to resist. We pretended it hadn't happened. I led Virginia to the car. This time, I buckled her first thing.

We drove a few miles before I stopped and turned off the engine. I reached into the back seat and grabbed her phone.

"I'm taking your phone with me. If I were your sister or a friend or something like that, I'd tell you to lose the dumbass. You're going to do what you want, but you deserve better. I'm sorry for the inconvenience. I'll leave the key for the cuffs on the dashboard."

"Thank you. You're right. You know, what you said before. I won't be able to go to the police. I see that now." She still didn't trust me.

"Count to three hundred before you take off your blindfold and leave. If you do that, you won't get hurt." I saw Rosa's headlights coming toward us.

"Starting now." I opened my door, put the key on the dashboard, and squeezed her shoulder.

"Bye, Virginia."

19

If my sister said anything, I didn't hear it. I got in Rosa's car, and we drove off.

"You scared me, Kell." Rosa gave me one of her looks and pantomimed wiping sweat off her brow.

"I'll never be that close to her again. I wanted her to know I existed, that we came from the same parents."

Rosa nodded. "But you can't."

"I know."

Rosa nodded at Virginia's phone. "What's that?"

"Her phone. I didn't want to run the chance that she'd call the cops first chance she got."

"Just make sure you get rid of it."

"I will."

We met Richard back at the hotel. He was all creepy smiles. "Ladies," he said, greeting us. He counted out our money. "It's been a pleasure. We'll have to do it again sometime. Any ideas about how you're going to spend your money?"

"Make a Costco run and get some snacks," Rosa said.

"Manicure and pedicure," I said.

Richard laughed. "Guess what I'm doing with mine? First, I'm getting my lady a boob job." He threw up his hands. "Hey, it's what she wants. Not my idea, even if I think it's an excellent one. Then we're going to Costa Rica for a few months."

"Send a postcard," Rosa said.

"You know I will."

Richard tried to talk Rosa and me into having sex, so he could watch us. He said it like it was a joke, but he offered us a thousand bucks apiece. We told him thanks, but no. We shook hands, and Rosa and I headed back to Georgia.

"Are you better off knowing?" Rosa asked. "Or would you have been better off not knowing?"

I leaned back in the car. "I needed to know. "

"You couldn't have killed her, could you? If you had to?" Rosa didn't let me answer. "That part of our lives is over. Neither of us can do it anymore. You understand that, don't you?"

I was quiet for so long, Rosa piped up again. "I hope you're thinking about the new line of work you're going into, Kell."

"Something happened that I didn't tell you about."

She glanced over.

"A cop came by," I said.

"To the beach house?"

"Yes. He was patrolling. Bored, I guess. I don't think I could have killed him. You have no idea how much that disappointed me. I couldn't do it because she would have known. I would have been ashamed."

"So what happened?"

"I tongue kissed him and told him to come back later."

Rosa laughed. "He'll always be looking for you."

"He was a kid. Easy to fool."

"Any chance he saw your license plate?"

"No. It was parked in back. He stayed in front. He'll never put it together."

"He'll come back for weeks trying to find you. He'll always think about you, what might have been. This guy we conned, he's not going to the police. There's too much to lose. More than money."

"She's going to leave him."

"She told you that."

"I could tell. I kept looking at her, wondering if I would have been more like her, or if she would have been more like me."

"People turn out the way they turn out." Rosa made a face. "I don't think your parents would be happy with me."

I laughed. What could I say?

"I'm heading in a different direction," Rosa said. "You should too. We've been lucky. You need to find something else. I don't want you to go back to vodka and Cocoa Puffs."

"I won't. I've come through that."

"By the way, who decorated your house?"

I smiled. I hadn't changed anything since I'd moved in. Rosa had helped me decorate my Chicago condo. We ended up going to auctions and flea markets. The result was eclectic and classy. The Stone Mountain house was neither.

"Didn't know you were into country," Rosa said.

"Everything came with the house. That's one thing I'll do. Redecorate."

"Good. You're young. You've got enough money. You could have any career you wanted."

"What are you going to do?"

"There's lots of foreclosures in Florida. We're thinking of buying, renovating, and then reselling. The market will come back. We'll be in a great position."

"Has Valerie given up her dream of going on archeological digs?"

Rosa looked over at me and then returned her gaze to the road. "Sweetie, that was part of the script. She has family in real estate. Commercial and residential."

"Oh." For some reason, it hurt. It wasn't the worst hurt I ever felt, but it stung. I didn't want to ask about the convent education. I still wanted that to be true. Rosa had said something earlier about not wanting Valerie and me to see each other. I couldn't figure out if it was because she was afraid we would kill each other or the opposite. Or both.

Rosa stayed one night at my house. We had sex, and it was fine.

"Are you in love with Valerie?" I asked later.

"Yes. I hope it lasts. I want it to. I'm in love with you too."

I laughed. "Just the two of us."

"She understands. Or says she does."

I figured Rosa was bullshitting me. I doubted she and Valerie had conversations about how she was in love with both of us, but it was sweet of her to say.

The next morning, I drove her up to the closest Waffle House. I couldn't convince her to try the grits, even when I ordered a bowl and put the spoon up to her mouth. Maybe next time. We ate our omelets and hash browns and laughed about Richard's idea of putting us on a TV show.

"The final scene of the pilot is us at the Waffle House," I said.

Rosa looked around. "I think it should be the final shot of every episode."

"Or the beginning," I said, thinking.

We debated this and never reached a conclusion.

Rosa had another serious discussion with me before she left. "Find something to keep busy," she said before she drove away. "Start working out again. Do something."

I nodded. I'd already made up my mind to go to the park every day. I hadn't climbed the mountain once since I'd moved to Georgia. In addition to hanging out at the park and redecorating, I'd figure out something.

"You look great," Nicole told me after I returned. "You must have had a good vacation."

I smiled and let her think what she wanted. Later, when she was watering containers by the pool, I casually said, "I visited my sister in California. She's a professor."

"That's cool. What does she teach?"

"Psychology. She has a Ph.D. She's the real deal. I hadn't seen her in a really long time."

"So you bonded again?"

I couldn't answer the question, so I stayed quiet.

"Whatever you did," she said, "you seem like you're in a better place."

"I am. It was cool to reconnect."

"You should get her to come down here."

I had. In a way. I'd kept Virginia's phone, despite my promise to Rosa. I regularly went through her photo gallery and saw pictures of people who were important to her. I tried to figure out the connections and felt pretty certain I'd identified her parents as well as her brothers. I also found a couple pictures of her dumbass boyfriend. He looked like a smug, rich boy. There were pictures, too, of other friends. It made me feel like I was part of her life.

Rosa called a week later. She and Valerie had bought a seriously distressed foreclosure property near South Beach. "It needs lots of work," Rosa said, "but we'll turn it into a showplace."

"Piece of cake, that's what it is," I said.

Meanwhile, I climbed the mountain every day. Sometimes I did it twice in a row. I also went to auctions and galleries and slowly got rid of the stuff that came with the house and replaced it with antiques and cool pieces that I liked.

After a few months, my clickety-clack brain came up with an interesting plan.

"Rosa," I said on the phone one night, "is it okay if I use your identity to take a college class?"

She was silent for a moment. I waited. "Why don't you use your own?" she finally asked.

I was ready for this. "I'm not sure what I want to major in. If I change my mind, I don't want this following me around."

"Are your credits too old to transfer? You could at least transfer in your core credits."

"I'm sure they're too old." I had no idea if they were or not.

"Mine are too, or I'd let you use my University of Chicago transcript. I don't see any problem with it. But, sweetie, no one is going to buy that you're in your mid-thirties."

"It's an online class. No face to face. No one will know how old I am. I mean, it'll be on my application, but—"

"Go ahead. What class are you taking?"

I laughed. "Believe it or not, I'm taking a psych course. I thought it might give me some insight into you."

She laughed too. "Good luck with that."

"I might study criminology again."

"Intriguing."

She didn't suspect a thing. I registered as Rosamunde Gold, ordered the textbook, and read it before class started.

I typed a short post to the teacher the morning the semester started: "Dr. Moorehead, I have been away from school for a long time, but I'm eager to begin again. I'm looking forward to learning from you. My past experiences have given me some interesting insights into psychology. Rosamunde (Rosa) Gold, Stone Mountain, GA"

She wrote back within an hour. "Hi, Rosa. I'm glad to hear you're interested in the class. Please feel free to share as much as you're comfortable with during the semester. By the way, I had a conference in Atlanta a few years ago and saw Stone Mountain for the first time. Marvelous! Best, Virginia Moorehead, Ph.D."

It was the equivalent of a form letter, but felt like a personal connection. I had been too afraid to use my real name. The chance was slight, but it was possible Virginia knew of me. There was also a chance, perhaps even smaller, that a Moorehead family member who knew about the adoption might see my name on her roster.

I figured I'd be able to write to my sister at least once a week, if not more often. As long as I didn't get stupid, I'd be okay.

Rosa would have a fit if she knew, but I had no plans to tell her. After all, I had done what she'd asked. I was keeping busy. I had already looked ahead to the next semester. Dr. Moorehead was teaching Personality Disorders. It sounded fucking interesting.

PART III

20

Three years later, I had a bachelor's degree in Psychology. I was in the graduate program at Oceanvue University, and Dr. Moorehead had finally convinced me to come to California for a semester so I could take an onsite class.

"It'll be good for you. I'm old-fashioned, Rosa. I think a real classroom is the best place to learn. Just one semester, and then you can go back to online classes to finish your master's," she'd written. "Think about the doctoral program down the road. You're an excellent student. I'd be happy to be your chair."

The truth was that I wanted to see her again. It'd be like a family reunion, only she wouldn't know it.

The bachelor's degree had been a piece of cake. The other required courses were okay. The only trouble I had was with a couple math classes. Math has never been my strength, but I called the real Rosa figuring accounting was essentially math. It was. She complained that she couldn't remember much, but Rosa turned out to be an ace student.

I had an absolute blast taking the psych courses with Dr. Moorehead. Don't get me wrong. It was challenging at times, but the more I interacted with her the more I liked her. She was funny, smart, caring, and a great teacher, passionate about her job. I worked my ass off in those classes, and she was pleased with my performance. One time I got a B+ on a paper about phobias. I had a meltdown. I asked if I could rewrite it. She told me not to worry about it, that I still had a strong A in the class, and to focus on the next assignments. I couldn't let it alone. I rewrote it and turned it in. She told me that she didn't usually change grades but would in this case.

I'd been in the graduate program for two semesters. In fact, I'd worked closely with Dr. Moorehead on several projects, and she'd put my name, along with some other grad students, on a couple papers she'd published.

I got to know her fairly well by reading her comments in the bulletin board section of the online class. She'd post questions or comments and get us involved in discussions. She didn't post a lot of personal information, but I learned that her mother was doing well. We were studying grief and dying, and Dr. Moorehead posted a short blurb about her mother being diagnosed with breast cancer and how she'd suffered from situational depression because of it. A bunch of students wrote and asked if her mother was okay now. She assured us that Mom was in great health.

Dr. Moorehead never specifically wrote about the kidnapping, but made several comments about being a crime victim. She made it sound like a violent crime, which I guess it technically was since I had a gun. I asked if the experience had made her less trusting. She posted that it had indeed made her less trusting and that she was still working through stuff. I also asked if it had changed her opinion about the justice system. "Ultimately no one can protect you if someone is intent on doing you harm, but I think the justice system does a good job. Without it, we'd have chaos." I feel exactly the same way.

Oceanvue was a quaint little town between Los Angeles and San Francisco with lots of beachfront. It was a college town and had a funky, punky vibe. There were lots of art galleries, coffee shops, and boutiques. In some ways, it reminded me of the town where I grew up, except we had a river and no university.

I moved into an extended stay hotel a week before classes started. The suite had a small kitchen and was clean and roomy. It had the feel of an upscale hotel room, and I figured I could stand it for a few months.

Obviously I was nervous about meeting Virginia face to face, afraid she'd recognize my voice. I'd picked up a slight southern accent while living in Georgia and decided to exaggerate it. I didn't sound like Daisy Duke, but hopefully I sounded different enough from her kidnapper to avoid getting caught.

I met Virginia in her campus office a few days before the semester started. Her office was on the main campus, the one that actually had an ocean view. It was a beautiful campus. Green lawns, Romanesque buildings, the ocean.

I easily found the department and waited for the student assistant to announce my arrival. Virginia came out and greeted me with a huge smile and a strong handshake. "It's great to meet you after all these years, Rosa."

She looked about the same. She'd put on a little weight and had different glasses, but I would have recognized her. She was still blonde, but her hair was cut in a more flattering style. She'd gotten hipper in the fashion department too. Another thing I noticed, she no longer wore the yin-yang necklace. Now she wore a simple gold chain. She'd also replaced the boring Timex with a chunky sports watch.

Virginia led me back to her office where we talked about the program and the classes I'd be taking. She had photos of her mom and dad on her desk. I recognized them from the phone gallery.

At the end of our meeting, she touched my hand. "I'm having a meet-and-greet at my house tonight. I hope you'll come."

Why not?

"You'll be able to meet some of your fellow graduate students," Virginia said. "Other faculty will be there too."

"Sounds like fun."

It was. Virginia lived in a neat mid-century beige brick ranch on Sedgwick. She'd decorated it with Eames and other modern furniture. They might have been knockoffs, but I got the feeling she had money.

Virginia introduced me to Larry Howell, who I assumed was her new boyfriend. She said he was an adjunct Criminal Justice instructor. Larry, was a big guy, tall, obviously a gym rat. Clean-shaven, he looked like a cop, not like the other academics. He didn't have a crew cut but close enough. I figured he did it because he was balding. I thought he might be scrutinizing me too much, so I tried to stay out of his line of sight.

Virginia had a delicious spread set up in her dining room with cheese, chips, bread, raw veggies, seafood, wine, beer, and soft drinks. I grabbed a cold Pepsi and a plate of stuff and was on my way to a corner when Virginia motioned me to rejoin her.

"This is Dr. Gretchen Wolf. She's my oldest friend," Dr. Moorehead said, introducing me to an attractive woman who'd just arrived.

Gretchen scrunched up her face. "She doesn't mean age-wise. I've known her since kindergarten."

I smiled and checked her out. I'd already seen her in the cell phone photos and had a teeny, tiny crush.

"She teaches composition courses at Oceanvue," Virginia said.

Virginia then introduced me to several other people, including Peter Taylor, Ingrid Birch, and Sandy Sherwood. They were in the graduate program with me. I'd taken online courses with them and felt an immediate reconnection with them. Peter could be snarky, but was smart. Ingrid was reasoned and mature. Sandy's comments were often laugh-out-loud funny, but she also had interesting insights. We were reminiscing about past classes when I caught Gretchen looking at me across the room. She smiled when I caught her eye. If I didn't know better, I'd think she was coming on to me. She turned, said something to Virginia, and laughed when my professor shot her a stern look. I thought for a moment, excused myself, and walked over to Gretchen.

She had long, curly reddish-brown hair. Her round face was intelligent, kind, and expressive. "I saw you looking at me and figured you wanted to fuck me." Well, I certainly didn't say that. This was, after all, Virginia's best friend.

"Do you teach graduate courses?" I asked.

"No. Just undergraduate. Actually mostly developmental."

She taught the slowpokes who weren't ready to take college-level courses. This was great news. There was no chance she'd be my instructor.

"I enjoy it," she added. "It's challenging, but I can make a difference."

"That's good. They need someone who's excited about it."

Her eyes twinkled. We smiled politely.

"You're only staying one semester?" she asked.

Virginia must have talked about me. I was flattered.

"Yes. I live in Georgia."

Virginia, who stood with Larry and several other professors, glanced over at us. She knew what the two of us knew. I was going home with Dr. Wolf.

21

I wondered how Gretchen would seduce me. She was a university professor who wanted to fuck a student. She had to handle this delicately. I almost rubbed my hands together in anticipation.

We'd gravitated away from everyone else and were now standing on the patio. The glass door leading to the living room was open. Gretchen occasionally glanced inside at Virginia, who was holding a wine glass, talking to Larry and a couple other people who I didn't know. I got the feeling that Gretchen was asking for permission.

We talked for a while about the upcoming semester. She inquired about my classes. I asked about hers. None of this had anything to do with what we really wanted. I found it fucking hilarious. I'm sure I smiled inappropriately at times. There were a couple times, too, when she giggled when there was really nothing worth chuckling about. Still, we had to do this dance.

I was enjoying myself. It had been a long time since I'd flirted.

"The beach is a couple blocks away," she said, leaning in like I might not be able to hear her. "Want to take a walk?"

Good move. We made our way out the front door without speaking to anyone. Gretchen must have gotten the permission she needed because I noticed no other check-ins with Virginia.

I heard and felt the ocean as we got closer. I breathed in deep.

I brushed against Gretchen several times before we reached the beach. She slid her hand into mine when we walked onto sand. I was ready to explode.

"Are you seeing anyone?" she asked, when we reached the pier.

"No." It was windy. I smoothed back my hair and held it with a fist. "I'm single." I was on the verge of making it easier for her by kissing her. "How about you?"

"Single. Gin says you're bright. She's real excited to have you in the program."

Gin. "That's good to hear."

"She doesn't say that about many people. Believe me."

I stayed quiet while she tried to get up her nerve. It was damn cute.

"Want to go back?" she asked.

"To?"

Gretchen hugged me. Her face was inches from mine.

"Is it okay if I kiss you?" she asked.

I'd never met anyone so fucking polite.

"Absolutely."

I left my car at Gin's and went home with Gretchen in her Subaru. She owned a renovated Victorian cottage a few blocks away. Gretchen had tons of artwork on the walls, mostly portraits of women. She also had lots of liberal political stickers and buttons on the refrigerator, PC, and a bulletin board in her office. I saw at least three "Impeach Bush" stickers, along with Clinton and Obama memorabilia.

I met her huge yellow cat named Bella and Thuggie, a little Shih Tzu mix. The cat was bigger than the dog, but they'd worked out an agreement.

To my great disappointment, Gretchen turned shy once we got to her house. She fed the critters and nervously started a conversation about the differences between undergraduate and graduate classes. I finally ran out of patience, pushed her against the wall, pulled down her jeans and panties, and got her off with my mouth. She led me to bed, and we went at it most of the night.

It was good. She was a little vanilla, but I wasn't complaining. I hadn't been a nun since Valerie, but I also hadn't been Chelsea Handler.

As I lay with Gretchen, I wondered if I would have slept with her if she hadn't been connected to Gin. I decided I would. It was great that she was her best friend, but I was attracted to her. She was my type. Long hair, curvy, funny, smart. I felt like I knew her because I'd looked at her picture dozens of times.

I wondered, too, if it was a good idea to get intimately involved in Gin's world. I had a vague, unsettled feeling but decided to ignore it. I'd be gone in a couple months. For now, I'd have some fun.

I was still in Gretchen's bed the next morning. In fact, I was asleep when the cell phone on the nightstand woke me. Gretchen hurried into the bedroom, mouthed 'sorry,' and answered it. She was already showered and dressed. I looked at a clock. It was after ten. She listened for a few moments and then said, "Uh, she's here."

With that, Gretchen walked out of the room, continuing her conversation in another room. I went on a scouting mission for my clothes and was dressed when Gretchen came back.

"That was Gin," she said. "She was worried about you. Your car is still in front of her house."

I smiled because Gretchen looked embarrassed. "Is she mad at you?"

"She was afraid she got you killed your first week in town."

Gretchen made a horrified face. "Her worst fear."

We started making out, and my clothes came off again. When we finally reached the point where we could keep our hands off each other, I showered, and Gretchen took me to pick up my car. I didn't see Gin which was fine. I'd see her in class in a couple days. I wanted to be a little more together, so I'd at least sound semi-intelligent. After too much sex, I can be mono-syllabic and sound like a stupid girl.

I dropped off my Mustang in the hotel parking lot, and Gretchen and I ate lunch at a deli on the beach.

"So you met Dr. Moorehead in kindergarten," I said. "Were your personalities already set?"

"I was pretty much the same." Gretchen mimicked someone happy, outgoing, cheerful. "Gin was shy. Well, she got over *that*. I call her Miss Bossy now."

We were sitting outside on a picnic table on a raised deck. It was sunny and breezy.

"Did she have any problem with you being gay?" I asked.

Gretchen shook her head. "Not at all. In fact, she was the one who told me. I agreed with her. Her parents were great too. Very supportive. She has a wonderful family. Nobody changed toward me when I came out."

"What do you think of her boyfriend?"

Gretchen made a face. "Larry's okay, I guess. She doesn't make the best choices in that department. We've both been kind of losers in that area."

It was the kind of thing that a person regrets the second it comes out, but once it's out, well, you've just got to make the best of it.

"I didn't mean that the way it sounded," she said, touching my hand.

I shrugged.

"I just meant that we don't usually approve of each other's partners," she said. "Wow. I can't seem to say the right thing. I'm going to shut up. Anyway, she's crazy about Larry, so I try to say supportive things."

"But you don't like him."

"He's kind of boring. Not his conversations. He can be interesting, but he sees the world in a different way. I think he might be Republican."

"Was he a cop?"

Gretchen shrugged. "Something with law enforcement. I can't remember."

"Was Dr. Moorehead surprised we went back to your place?"

"No." Gretchen gave a short laugh. "Not that I—"

"I'm your type?"

"It's not that so much. She could see the vibe going on between us. Then we disappeared. She figured we didn't go to the library."

"You have anything planned for today?" My classes didn't start for two days.

"Not a thing. I've done most of my prep work for next semester."

We went back to her house and played the weekend away.

When I went to my first class with Dr. Moorehead on the following Monday, she was pleasant but didn't shoot me a wink or anything like that. She and Gretchen talked on the phone every day, so I figured she knew her best friend and I had been together since we'd met.

By the end of the week, I was living at Gretchen's. I didn't give up the hotel room, but I spent every night at her place. I handled her inevitable questions about my background by telling her that I was an only child and hadn't been in contact with my parents in a long time. She didn't pry.

I almost screwed up a couple times. Once I was on the verge of asking Gretchen if she'd traveled to China with Gin.

Another time I almost asked about the yin-yang necklace. I was curious about it. I had a suspicion it had been a gift from Mike.

All in all, it was a challenge to do my coursework, have a relationship with Gretchen, and lie about my personal details. Sometimes I wondered if I hadn't gotten myself in too deep. Even a small misstep, I knew, could lead to disaster.

22

"Were you raised Jewish?" Gretchen asked.

When I chose to use Rosa's name, it never occurred to me that it identified me as Jewish to a whole bunch of people. Gretchen and I were eating at a little restaurant near campus called Mimi's. It was a deli, and I'd ordered a whitefish salad sandwich on a French roll. I was about to take a bite when she asked the question. It suddenly occurred to me that Gretchen often took me to delis.

She must have thought that she offended me in some way because she looked away.

"Uh—" I had to do some scrambling here. I didn't know enough to fake it. I had no idea if Gretchen was Jewish. I was afraid if I said I'd been raised in the faith, she'd come up with another question that was beyond my scope.

"No, I wasn't," I said. "My parents weren't religious. I don't know much about religion." I paused. "We were non-practicing." Isn't that what it's called? I hoped so. After that, she wanted to leave the whole religion thing alone. Thank God.

Gretchen was amazingly chatty about Gin. I think she sometimes forgot that Gin was my professor. It wasn't long before she told me about the kidnapping.

"You can't ever tell anyone about this," she warned one day when we were eating pizza on her back porch. I promised. "I'm serious. She'd kill me if she knew I told you." I promised again.

She told me that she and Gin used to call Mike 'Dildo' for obvious reasons. The relationship was horrible, based only on sex, and Gin had never told her family about it.

"Gin has an inferiority complex," Gretchen said. "Her brothers are younger. Harlan has a Ph.D. in Chemical Engineering. Drew has one in Theoretical Physics. They're both married, and at the time had published two books apiece. When the kidnapping happened, Harlan was already a full professor at the University of Texas, and Drew was close to getting tenure at Stanford. Gin had a Ph.D. in Psychology and was an assistant professor at a mid-level research university with no books to her credit, though she was trying to turn her dissertation into one—and had been trying for two years. She felt like she had a big 'L' written on her forehead. Anyway, she chooses guys who are losers. I guess so she'll feel superior."

I chewed my sandwich and took a swig of Dr. Brown's Black Cherry. Frankly, this smacked of dime store psychology to me, but I hung on Gretchen's every word.

"After Mike, she didn't date until she met Larry," Gretchen said. "We call him Mr. Black-and-White because that's how he sees the world. Anyway, after she got kidnapped, she and Mike broke up."

I tried not to ask too many questions about the kidnapping, but was, of course, curious. "Was she freaked out for a long time afterwards?"

"I asked if she wanted to go to counseling," Gretchen said. "I figured she might have post-traumatic stress from it, but she said she was fine. I think more than anything she felt stupid. She was embarrassed. It made her realize that she was with the wrong guy and made really bad decisions. It's funny, but she turned the kidnapping into a kind of cottage industry. It energized her career. She finished her book. Since then, she's written a bunch of papers, and now she's working on a new book about violent female criminals. She's one of the biggest experts in the world."

Life is fucking ironic, isn't it? "What happened to Mike?"

"He went back to his wife. The weird part, though, is that he was convinced—or at least he told Gin he was—that his wife was behind the whole thing."

"But he went back to her."

"I know. Oh, and he got religion or says he did. He went all churchy. They don't have any contact. Get this. Before he told Gin he thought his wife was behind it, he told her he thought *she* was behind it. Apparently he saw some photos he swore were of her. The photos made it look like she was dead. He actually accused her of posing for the photos."

"What did she say?"

"Wooh! Let's just say she quickly disavowed him of that notion. She was livid that he'd accuse her after what she'd been through."

"Did she think about going to the police?"

Gretchen snorted. "No. Mike offered her money not to. She didn't take it, of course. She figures the whole thing cost him a lot of money. He comes from money, so I guess he had it. He's a loser, but his dad owns a car place. When she first got kidnapped, it didn't occur to her that it was connected to Mike. She was worried her parents or the university would have to pay a ransom. That didn't really compute. So then she thought she got kidnapped by mistake. She said the kidnapper told her she was a lesbian." Gretchen usually made more sense than this, but she was struggling to remember everything.

I made a face. "Why would the kidnapper feel the need to point that out?"

Gretchen shrugged. "I don't know. Maybe she was coming on to her." She laughed. "I asked if she got her number. I was a little desperate at the time." Her face clouded. "She told Gin that she was a professional killer. God, can you imagine?"

"Not really."

"She probably did it to scare her. It did."

I kept my mouth shut.

Gretchen was on a roll. "Gin thought the kidnapper was going to take her somewhere in the car, shoot her, and dump her, so she did everything she could to bond with her. Gin even told her about her mom's breast cancer. Psychologically, she knew the more human she seemed the better she'd be treated. She said she started crying, and the kidnapper tried to comfort her."

"She was really crying or faking it?"

"Really crying. She started sobbing. Kind of lost it. So the kidnapper came over and touched her head and rubbed her back."

"She doesn't sound so bad."

"Well, it kind of pissed off Gin. For one thing, Gin doesn't like to cry in front of people. It embarrassed her. For another— she didn't say this—but I think that she was afraid the kidnapper was coming on to her. You know, a comforting pat followed by a feel up. She thought it was weird that the woman told her she was gay."

"Maybe the things the kidnapper told her weren't true. If the kidnapper was worried about being caught, she'd probably give her disinformation. I would."

Gretchen nodded. "You're right." She winked. "I'd like to think that she was a lesbian though. Don't tell her I told you this—I'm serious—but it kind of kinkified Gin."

I wasn't sure which question to ask.

"Do you want another soda?" Gretchen asked.

"No, thanks."

"She didn't go gay or anything like that, but she's kind of gotten into—" Gretchen waved her hands.

"What?" Yeah, it was none of my business, but I asked. You would too. You know you would.

"Uh, role playing, getting tied up."

"With Mr. Black-and-White?" I asked.

"Yeah. Apparently he's not so black-and-white in bed."

That was more than I needed to know. "You two talk about everything, don't you?"

"Oh, yeah."

"What do you say about me?"

Gretchen blushed. "Nothing like that. Just things we do."

"Except that."

"Never that."

"What's my nickname? You named Mike 'Dildo.' Larry is 'Mr. Black-and-White.'" I gave her a look. "You don't really expect me to believe that I don't have a nickname."

Gretchen blushed and covered her face. She moaned.

"What is it?" I asked.

She didn't want to tell me. "Miss Hottie," she finally said.

"It could be worse."

"Oh, it could be a *lot* worse. You wouldn't believe what Gin has called some of my girlfriends. Anyway, Gin kept track of information about the kidnapper, so she could maybe help identify her after she was released." Gretchen thought for a moment. "She thought she had a Midwestern accent. She said she was a lesbian. She was a smoker. She was probably obsessive-compulsive because she had a thing about clean bathrooms. She said she was a professional killer. She said her parents died in an accident. Something happened when she was sixteen. I can't remember the other things. Something about her parents and cooking—She knew information about Gin and her family. She asked Gin questions about her brothers."

"Like what?"

"If she liked them."

"That's strange."

"Yeah," Gretchen said. "Gin figured that she might have some kind of personality disorder because some of the questions didn't make sense within the context."

"I'm guessing someone who kidnaps someone probably has a personality disorder."

Gretchen laughed. "You're right. She looked into research on professional killers. Apparently that's an under-researched field. She looked at research on serial killers, but that didn't fit at all."

"A professional killer isn't really a serial killer."

"That's what she decided."

"For one thing, one of them does it for money," I said. "It's a career. The other one does it because he or she likes it. Maybe has a compulsion to kill."

"She decided they had more differences than similarities."

"Did she think about studying professional killers?" I asked.

"No. Too dark. Not that serial killers aren't, but she didn't want to go there. Plus, the woman might have lied about it."

"I think she did. I don't know a whole lot about it, but I don't see hiring a professional killer to kidnap someone. It seems like different skill sets."

"That's exactly what she thought," Gretchen said.

"She probably said she was a professional killer to keep her in line."

"It worked. Oh, the kidnapper also said she got shot in the head. I don't know how I forgot that."

"Shot in the head?"

"Yeah. And then something about how that wasn't the worst thing that happened to her."

Gretchen pinched off a couple pieces of her crust to give to Thuggie later.

"Maybe she said weird things because she had a brain injury," I said.

"Maybe. Gin figured the blindfold was used partly because the scar was noticeable, and it would have been easy to identify her."

I shuddered, letting Gretchen think that I imagined a horribly disfigured woman. The scar from Valerie's shooting was minimal and mostly hidden by my hair. If Gretchen noticed it, she'd never asked me about it.

"The real mystery, though, is what the kidnapper said when she got the final phone call before she let Gin go," Gretchen said.

"Go on," I said, pretending I didn't know the story.

"She said something like, 'You called at a good time. I almost told her.'"

"To the person on the other line?"

"Yes."

"Told her what?"

"Gin doesn't know," Gretchen said. "She's tried to figure it out.

I pretended to be deep in thought. "Does she have *any* idea?"

"None. We've both tried to figure it out."

"Maybe it was about who was really behind it. Maybe it *was* the wife."

Gretchen shook her head. "That doesn't make sense."

"People do strange things. Maybe the wife wanted to punish him for cheating."

"That's a lot of money to lose," Gretchen said. "She could have just paid to have him beaten up. That would have been a lot cheaper."

"So when you talk to Dr. Moorehead, do you actually refer to me as 'Miss Hottie?'"

Gretchen was mortified. "Not all the time."

"That's my professor."

"I know. She tells me the same thing. 'She's my student, Gretch.' Sometimes I forget. Sorry."

I was enrolled in a Special Topics (Psychology of Violence) class with Gin as well as Independent Study. The cool thing was that I could use much of what I did in Independent Study for papers in my Special Topics class. Gin suggested I interview women prisoners who'd been convicted of violent crimes for my Independent Study. The interview questions were ones that Gin had developed with another researcher who worked at a college in Oregon. I hesitated when Gin suggested it. I wasn't exactly keen on going *inside* a women's prison. Her eyes had lit up, though, when she told me about it. Despite my misgivings, I didn't want to disappoint her.

Once a week, I drove to Valley State Prison in Chowchilla. Some inmates shot me a look like they knew I should be in there with them, but no one was uncooperative or ugly with me, and I found the research fascinating.

There was one inmate in particular who got to me. Carla Santo was about my age but looked twenty years older. She was serving life for an armed robbery that went bad. A convenience store clerk had been shot to death. Carla told me several times that she didn't pull the trigger. Maybe she did, and maybe she didn't. Her boyfriend testified against her, and the jury bought it. She got life, and he got twenty years. He was already out. She wouldn't be up for parole for another ten years.

I'd had lots of breaks along the way. Carla hadn't had any, except bad ones. I was a total idiot when I first started and could easily have been put in prison. If I'd been incarcerated, I'd probably look like Carla. Pale, metallic, scarecrow-like. Sometimes I had the feeling when I talked to her that she was on to me. She never said anything, but occasionally raised an eyebrow or squinted her eyes.

I wasn't supposed to go off script during the interviews. Gin warned me that prisoners would try to work me, that it was best to stay structured. For the most part, I followed Gin's instructions. However, sometimes I let Carla talk because she needed to. Her voice was like sandpaper, and she was difficult to understand. Her teeth were in bad shape, and she was self-conscious, so she'd cover her mouth when she smiled. One time, I asked if there was anything she wanted me to bring her. She covered her mouth and said, "Yeah, Rosa, bring me a fucking time machine. Let me go back in time and do things differently. Will you do that for me? Will you bring that to me, honey?" She said it in a dramatic tone that was kind of scary. I didn't know what to say, so I told her I'd pick one up at Walmart. She laughed and said, "Shit."

Gin was happy with my research and kept telling me that she wanted me to apply to the doctoral program. I was enjoying myself. The whole academic thing was like solving puzzles. I was thinking I could get a doctoral degree and maybe continue researching violent women criminals. Maybe one day I'd be internationally known like Gin.

I'd figure out the logistics later. Everything I did at school was under Rosa's name and social security number. I'd worry about fixing anything that needed to be fixed when the time came.

In addition to the classes with Gin, I took a Quantitative Research Methodology class. It was a fancy title for statistics. The class was kicking my ass. I asked Gretchen if she could tutor me, but she threw up her hands and said, "I'm all Language Arts. I can't do math or science." I didn't want to ask Gin because I didn't want her to think I was a Dumbassian.

I ended up calling or emailing Rosa a couple times a week to bail me out. Bless her heart, she thought I was still in Georgia.

My statistics professor, Dr. Dornan, couldn't explain things in a way that made sense to me. That's what Gin said when I told her that I didn't think he was earning his salary. He might be a smart guy—she assured me he was—but he was a loser as a teacher. Fortunately, Rosa was an excellent teacher and said things in a way that made me say, "Oh, I get it." I kept telling Rosa that she'd missed her calling. She said, "Yeah, yeah, yeah. I should have been a college professor." Anyway, she took a real interest in the class and often asked, "So how we'd do on that last quiz?" She'd forgotten that it really was 'we' since it was all in her name.

23

It didn't take long before I became a member of Gretchen's household. I did laundry, picked up groceries, vacuumed, walked Thuggie and took him to the groomer. I even mowed the lawn and gave pills to Bella. Do you have any idea how difficult it is to give a three hundred pound cat a pill? I've had easier hits.

I also washed the cars. Gretchen liked to watch me from inside the house. "I'll gladly pay you a hundred bucks to wash my car," she liked to tell me.

Gretchen was a vegetarian and had been since high school. I thought she was joking when she told me. "Don't worry," she said, "I'm not going to turn you into one." That was a fucking relief. "Thuggie and Bella are still carnivores. I haven't tried to convert them." The funny thing was that after several weeks, I hardly ate meat at all, except for fish.

Gretchen and I were compatible. We had fun together, even when we weren't fucking. She liked foreign films, and though I never thought I'd like them, it turned out I did. At least most of them. There were a few German ones that made me fall asleep. I also liked most of the TV shows she watched. They were of the PBS or Discovery Channel variety, and viewing them resulted in lively discussions. The good news was that I wasn't bored out of my fucking mind.

We saw Gin socially at least once a week. It was often just the three of us. Most Saturday mornings we met her at Katz's for coffee and bagels. One time, we got together with her to bowl. It was my idea. Maybe it was crazy, but the inside joke appealed to me. I mentioned to Gretchen that I thought it might be cool to bowl, and she organized an outing. It was a blast—no one was good, but that was part of the fun. We agreed to do it again soon.

It would be easy to be intimidated by their Ph.D.s, but Gin and Gretchen were like everyone else. They giggled and carried on, expressed frustration with students and administrators, and got excited about stimulating classes and discussions. They were especially goofy when they were together, trying to make each other laugh.

I'd brought some pot with me from Georgia. Gretchen's eyes lit up when I showed it to her.

"Will Gin get high with us?" I asked.

Gretchen vehemently shook her head. "Not with you. That's a line she will not cross. She would never, ever, ever get high with one of her students."

"Does she get high?"

Gretchen hesitated which answered my question as far as I was concerned. I smiled. "What about Mr. Black-and-White?" I asked.

She nodded.

"I figured," I said. "He strikes me as a big hypocrite."

"But neither would get high with a student. In fact, Gin's not totally comfortable socializing with you as much as she does."

This hurt my feelings. Was she just putting up with me because of Gretchen?

"She doesn't think it's right to socialize with students too much," Gretchen explained. "She believes in boundaries. She's afraid someone will think she treats you different because you're friends. She thinks about ethics a lot."

Gin had recently begun hugging me goodbye. I would never

have initiated something like that, but I was thrilled she had. Dad used to tell me that I had a bit of the devil in me, and there were times when I wondered what would happen if I whispered, "Have a good life," in her ear. Obviously I'd have to be a fucking moron to fuck up what I had, so I was able to control myself.

I toyed with the idea of staying another semester. Nicole Westlake was taking care of the Stone Mountain property, so I didn't have to worry about the house.

Life was good in Oceanvue until it wasn't. I think it started to go bad when I went to the anniversary party for Gin's parents.

"The Mooreheads are celebrating their thirty-fifth anniversary," Gretchen announced one day. "We're invited to the party."

This was risky. Gin's parents might recognize me. Maybe I resembled one of my parents or Gin enough to make them suspicious. Another concern I had was that Larry would be there. I had done pretty well at avoiding him. I was not, to say the least, comfortable around law enforcement. To make matters worse, Gretchen's parents and sister would be at the party too. Yikes.

Gretchen assumed that I would go. In order to avoid a confrontation, I pretended it was fine and dandy with me. "Great," I said. "I'm looking forward to it." For that line alone, I should have received a fucking Oscar nomination.

The Mooreheads lived in a small suburb close to Los Angeles. Their house was a sprawling Spanish-style ranch with a beautiful garden and pool in the backyard.

"Did Gin grow up here?" I asked Gretchen when we arrived.

"Mostly. They moved here when she was a baby. It's the only house she remembers."

Larry and Gin had already arrived. Gin introduced me to her brothers and their families and then to her parents. I carefully watched Mrs. Moorehead's eyes when we were introduced.

"Mom, this is Rosa Gold," Gin said. "She's in the graduate program." She didn't add that I was living with Gretchen, but I got the feeling Mrs. Moorehead knew because she glanced at Gretchen and smiled.

"Call me Edith, Rosa." She shook my hand and didn't seem to notice that I shared her daughter's genes. Edith, a plump woman whose long graying hair was piled on her head, oozed lots of maternal warmth.

Gin's dad was a short, round bald-headed guy with a firm handshake. "Fred," he said by way of introduction. He also didn't get that Gin and I were related. I guess if you're not looking for it, you don't see it. He was gruff but amiable. Maybe they were faking it, but the Mooreheads seemed like a genuinely pleasant family.

"Rosa, these are my parents, Russ and Yvette Wolf. And my sister Jill." One thing I knew for sure, Gretchen wasn't adopted. Gretchen had her mother's curly hair, and her father's moon face. Jill looked like a straight version of Gretchen.

"This is Rosa Gold," Gretchen said.

I was warmly greeted and even got a hug from Jill. "I feel like I know you," she said. "Gretchen's talked so much about you."

"All good," Gretchen quickly added.

"Of course," Jill said, laughing.

"Come to our house soon for dinner," Yvette Wolf said with a slight accent. Gretchen had told me her mother was French and had been a flight attendant. Her dad had been a pilot, and they'd met on a flight.

"We'd love to have you over, Rosa," Russ said.

Everyone was so pleasant it made me feel guilty. I wasn't exactly using Gretchen, but they wouldn't have been so accommodating if they knew what a fucking liar I was.

I tried my best to stay away from Larry. He met my gaze a couple times, but I quickly broke it. I wasn't sure if he was picking up on the resemblance between Gin and me or if he had an instinctual sense that I was a criminal. Whatever it was, the big gorilla rattled me.

There was an awkward moment late in the day when the time came for photographs. There were several taken with Gin, her brothers, and parents. Other combinations were then photographed. Gin pulled in Gretchen. Gretchen motioned for me to join her.

I felt like everyone stopped what they were doing to stare at me. I had two problems. One, would anyone look at the photo somewhere down the road and see the resemblance? Second, was I ready to stand next to Gretchen and indicate to the world that we were a couple? I hesitated. This was a no-win situation. If I didn't join Gretchen, I'd embarrass her and catch hell later. Were we a couple? Was I ready to make that statement? If I wasn't, did I really want to have the, "You don't think of us as a couple" argument? If you've never had it, trust me, it's not fun. You end up getting yelled at and have zero sex for a while. I'd rather give a pill to Bella. Gin shot me a look that suggested I needed to do the right thing and stand next to Gretchen. Fuck it. I stood next to Gretchen.

I could have sworn Larry looked at me, then Gin, and back at me. Over and over. Maybe I was paranoid. Gretchen squeezed my hand and whispered an inappropriate sexual comment in my ear. She'd been doing it most of the day, but this one was really filthy. After a couple months with me, she wasn't so vanilla anymore. Her comment made me laugh. That's when they took the photo.

I looked over at Larry. He stared at me, arms folded.

While most partygoers stayed outside in the garden and pool area, I wandered into the house to snoop. I was drawn to the family photos in the living room. Photographs were apparently a big deal because there were tons of them. I zeroed in on Gin's childhood shots. I couldn't help but smile. As a kid, she looked remarkably like me. We'd both been skinny with similar facial expressions. Her hair, like mine, had been brown. She didn't stick out like a sore thumb in the family portraits, but if you looked closely you could see a clearer resemblance between Harlan and Drew and the parents.

There were also photos of Edith and Fred when they were first married. Both were much thinner. Edith had long, straight dark hair that parted in the middle. Fred had a mustache and longish hair down to his collar.

A group of photo albums stretched across one bookshelf near the television. I wondered if there were photos of my parents. I was tempted to start looking when Gin and Larry walked in, carrying drinks.

"Good looking family," I said.

Gin cringed. "You're not looking at those, are you?"

"Did your hair turn blonde or—" I knew the answer but played dumb.

"I started coloring it in college. You didn't hear that, Larry. He thinks I'm a natural blonde."

"This obsession women have with coloring their hair," Larry said. "Maybe I should color mine." He rubbed his sparse hair. "You ever think about going blonde, Rosa?"

I hesitated. It seemed an innocent enough question, certainly within the context of our conversation, but it scared the hell out of me. Did he know? How could he? Richard might not have destroyed the motel photos. He was a doofus, and might have shown them to someone. Had Larry seen them? Maybe Richard had been arrested. I couldn't ask Rosa because she'd wonder what I was up to.

Gin turned to me because I hadn't answered. She seemed to be picturing me blonde.

"Seems like too much trouble," I said. "One of those things that once you do it, you have to keep doing it. I'm not sure it's a good look for me anyway."

"Gretchen was the one who got me to do it," Gin said. "I was in college and got my heart broken by this guy I'd been dating since high school. I wanted to do something drastic, so she told me to color my hair. Here we are."

"Did it change your life?" Larry asked.

Gin laughed. "Yes," she said. "It did. That's a story for another day."

Larry stared at the photos. "I'm trying to decide which of your parents you look most like," he said.

I couldn't look at him.

"I guess Mom," Gin said, gazing at the photos.

She didn't have a clue that she was adopted. Larry looked at me. "What do you think, Rosa?" he asked.

"I'm not good at that kind of thing," I said, walking away.

I heard them murmur something, but I couldn't make it out.

When I found Gretchen near the pool, I was thinking how weird it was that I was able to walk among all these people who knew the Moorehead family so well, and no one picked up on the fact that Gin and I were sisters. It must be the name. They hear Rosa Gold. Something happens in their heads. They probably wouldn't notice if Gin and I were identical twins.

Most of the guests surrounded Harlan and wife Becky. They had a new baby, Sofia, and people were going crazy over her.

Gretchen was talking to Jill and her parents. I wasn't eager to join the conversation, but I wanted to escape Larry.

"We're serious about the invitation, Rosa," Russ said.

Yvette nodded. "You're always welcome," she said.

"Gretchen said you like to bowl," Jill said. "Maybe we can get together and do that."

"That'd be great," I said.

"We'll do something when the semester ends," Gretchen said. "We're both busy right now, but once we get a break, I promise we'll get together."

Finally, the day drew to a close. Gretchen and I headed back to Oceanvue.

"My family liked you." Gretchen chuckled. "That doesn't usually happen. They haven't liked most of my girlfriends. They've been on Gin's side."

"Jeez, Gretchen, who have you brought home?"

She cleared her throat. "Have you decided if you're going to stay next semester?"

Uh-oh. She was gearing up for the "talk."

"I'm thinking about it. Do you want me to?" I shouldn't have asked.

"Yes," she said, turning to look at me. "I would love for you to stay at least one more semester." Gretchen glanced at the road and then back at me. "I'm not trying to pressure you." That was a good thing because the kind of person I am, well, I'd just run the other way.

"Just think about it," she said. "Gin's real happy with you. She's grooming you for a Ph.D. You've got a great situation here. She's willing to guide you through the program, Rosa."

It was mind boggling when I stopped to think about it. My name was Rosa, I was enrolled in a graduate program in Psychology, and I was on the verge of getting married. How long could I keep this up?

I'd reached the conclusion that, like most things, academia was a big fucking game. It was a racket filled with phonies who weren't necessarily good at teaching or research but knew how to play the game to get promotions and awards. Gretchen liked to say that there was nothing more political than an academic department. Maybe it'd turn out to be the perfect place for me.

"If you stay," Gretchen said, "I was thinking you might as well give up the hotel room. Unless it's important for you to keep it for some reason." She was treading lightly but progressing rapidly. Getting her family's approval sealed the deal for her. She giggled. "I'm not scaring you, am I? I'm not trying to. If I'm moving too fast, just say so."

That's what she said, but I'd been around long enough to know that if I said, "You're moving too fast," it was never the right thing to say. If I stayed, I was perfectly content to go on with Gretchen. Even if I didn't, if I returned to Georgia, I was considering a long-distance romance. Things were good between us. Other than the little fact that our relationship was based on a total lie.

That night, after we had sex, Gretchen finally said it. "I love you." I'd figured out a long time ago that there was only one right answer to this. Just fucking say it because if you don't you're going to get trapped in a conversation you don't want.

"I love you too, babe."

The words made her happy. I was pleased, too, because I'd dodged another bullet.

24

"That one by Brent and Baum is interesting. I'm not sure I agree with it, but the findings are intriguing." I handed Gin a folder of research articles she'd asked me to photocopy.

I liked hanging out in Gin's office. It was on the second floor of Herndon Hall in a building that still had lots of 1920s character like marble floors and oak staircases.

Gin was more relaxed here than in class, and it was usually just the two of us. It wasn't an attractive office, but Gin made it comfortable by adding an Oriental rug, lamps, artwork, and bookshelves. Soft classical music played from a small stereo on the shelves. The room, like Gin, had a good vibe.

She gazed at the Brent and Baum article. It was about women prisoners and the role that social support played within prisons. "Is that right?" she asked. "Do you want a cup of coffee?" She motioned to the Mr. Coffee machine on the window sill. I helped myself to a cup and a Mint Milano cookie from the Pepperidge Farm bag.

"I got the feeling they didn't ask the right questions," I said, taking a bite of the cookie.

She motioned for me to continue and then picked at cookie crumbs on the white paper plate in front of her. She maintained eye contact and appeared interested in my opinion. One of the things that I liked best about Gin was her intensity. When you discussed something with her, she was engaged and thinking all the time.

"For one thing, they never reported how the prison cells were set up," I said. "Were the women able to have conversations with other inmates? They also didn't report on any structured events set up by the prisons. Did they offer activities? You know, stuff like that."

"Sloppy research."

I shrugged. "You might read it differently."

She smiled. "Thanks for doing this. What did you think about last night's class?"

"I thought it was great."

She put up a hand. "I'm not looking for compliments, Rosa. I mean, what did you think about what Peter said about women and hormones?"

I laughed. Psychology of Violence was a small class, and males were definitely in the minority. Still, Peter felt the need to pipe up and make the comment that hormonal women could be just as violent as men with too much testosterone. "I think it was an ill-conceived statement to make to that particular audience," I said.

"I'm pre-menstrual," Gin said, running her hand through her hair. "If Larry made a comment like that, I'd have violent ideation. I've often wondered how women live together. Are you and Gretchen ever hormonal at the same time?"

I shook my head. "It hasn't been a problem."

Gretchen and I got along fine. Occasional moments of tension were usually dissolved with a joke or other humor. If that didn't work, I got in my car, drove around, and returned as though nothing had happened. Gretchen never pushed it.

"By the way, did she do a polish on your last paper?" she asked. Before I had a chance to answer, she frantically waved her hand. "Don't worry. I'm not upset if she did. She polishes my papers too. I thought I recognized her work."

"She did."

"It's fine. Really. She's a fantastic editor. You'd be a fool not to use her. What about next semester? Have you decided if you're staying?"

"I've been thinking about it."

Gin nodded approvingly.

"Maybe take one class online and two onsite," I said. "What are you teaching?"

"I'm doing a couple undergraduate courses, but I'm also doing a methods class in qualitative research. You could take it and continue your research at the prison."

I thought about it. Qualitative research was the opposite of statistics. It included interviews and living among populations in order to gather subjective data.

"In fact, you could do an ethnographic study where you'd spend most of the day with the prisoners," she said.

I swallowed. That might be too close for comfort for me.

Gin must have sensed my discomfort. "It could be kind of scary, I guess, but, wow, you could do some killer research." She smiled at the play on words. "Seriously, you could compile some outstanding data. Do you think you can handle it?"

I shrugged.

"Think about it," she said. "It might be exciting."

"Yeah. Exciting."

She immediately made a face as though something was troubling her. "Rosa, I wanted to ask you something."

I may have reddened. I probably stiffened. Something was up, and I was unprepared for it.

"First, is everything okay?" she asked. "Is the semester going all right?" She glanced away, adjusted a pile of papers, and looked at me again.

"Everything's fine." I folded my hands and sat up straighter.

"Good. I think I can get you grant money to help on the

research. I'll need a couple things though. For some reason, the state now requires a copy of a birth certificate along with your original social security card. Could you get those to me within a couple weeks?"

I felt cold. Trapped too. Gin had a difficult time looking at me. She pretended to look through the folder of photocopies. Her brow furrowed, but she wasn't thinking about the articles. I searched my brain for why she'd need a birth certificate and social security card. Nothing came to mind.

"To be honest," I said, "someone else should probably get the money. I appreciate it, but I'm not in financial need."

"Oh." She'd probably never known a graduate student who didn't need money. "You're great at research. I wish I could compensate you."

"It's okay. Someone else needs the money more than I do."

"I've never asked you—How did you get interested in research on women criminals?"

We stared at each other. Where the fuck was this coming from? "I honestly don't remember," I said.

"Something you read?" she coaxed. "Someone you knew?"

I shrugged. "I don't think I was all that interested until I took classes with you. I think it was *you* who got me interested. You talked about your research when I took the Abnormal Psych class."

"That's right. I did." She smiled and glanced at the clock. "I've got to get to class. Larry and I are going up to Buster's tonight for dinner. Do you and Gretchen want to join us? Say around seven? We can't stay out late because I've got a morning class."

"I'll mention it to Gretchen, but I planned on studying. I've got a statistics exam I'm worried about."

"You've got to take a break sometime."

I hesitated. The last thing I wanted was to spend time with Larry. "I guess," I said.

That's how we all ended up together at Buster's Burgers that night. It was a university hangout that served burgers and beer in what had once been a gas station. The food was pretty good, but the place got loud and busy on the weekends. Tonight was a weeknight, however, and the place was quiet and only half full.

Larry and Gin were already seated at one of the round wood tables when we arrived. Larry stood, smiled real big, shook my hand, and hugged Gretchen.

Gin adored him. She often held his shirt sleeve or stroked his arm. Frankly, I didn't get why she was with him. Larry wasn't dumb, but he wasn't in Gin's league. Maybe it was physical.

Gin must have put a bug in his ear about engaging me. He asked about my classes, the differences between Georgia's climate and California's, whether I liked cats or dogs more, and several other questions that seemed ham-handed efforts to have a conversation with me. Frankly, it was creepy. Finally, when he asked about the mileage I was getting with my Mustang. I sighed and rolled my eyes.

Gretchen was perplexed by the battery of questions. None of the questions were particularly invasive, but I felt I was on the spot.

"Let her eat her sandwich," Gretchen said in a tone that indicated she meant it. "Gosh, Larry, you're full of questions tonight. Tell us what's going on with you. What are you teaching this semester?"

"A course on forensics and evidence," he said. "It involves lots of field work. Rosa, I think you'd enjoy it. Does she get to take any electives?" he asked Gin.

"Sure, if it pertains to her major," she said. "We could probably make an argument—"

"I'd rather take another research methods," I said. "Maybe Advanced Qualitative Methods. Dr. Moorehead and I talked about it earlier today."

"I misunderstood," Larry said. "I thought you were interested in criminology."

"Not really," I said.

Larry made a sound that indicated puzzlement. We ate our burgers and fries in tense silence. Gretchen and I had ordered black bean burgers. Mine was dry. I put more mayonnaise on it. It was a bad idea to come out tonight.

"How did you learn about Gin's research?" Larry asked.

"In class," I said.

"I mean, before you signed up," Larry said.

I stopped eating. "I didn't. I registered—"

"Right," he said. "But why did you register for her class? Weren't there several sections to choose from? Other professors you could have taken?"

I shrugged. "Just signed up," I said. "It was more than three years ago. It's hard to—I think it was the luck of the draw. I don't remember specifically choosing her."

"I can't remember what I did yesterday," Gretchen said in support.

Larry looked at Gin. "I thought you said she knew your research and decided to study with you."

Gin looked puzzled. "I don't remember saying that or knowing it. I honestly can't remember."

"Hmm. It doesn't matter," Larry said. He grabbed a handful of fries with his mitt of a hand and put them in his mouth.

"You working on any interesting cases, Larry?" Gretchen asked. "In your consulting business?" Her words had a tone. She wanted him to back off. I hoped he'd take the hint.

"Quiet time, actually," he said.

I was beginning to hate Larry. He was ruining everything. He was a jackass, probably a phony too. Had he figured out something about me, or was I being paranoid again?

"Rosa," Larry began.

I braced myself.

"You've worked with Gin on her research," he said. "What do you think is the most surprising fact in the research?"

This was a good professor-student question. Maybe he was just trying to include me.

"Wait," he said. "Let me rephrase that. Was there anything in the research that hit home with you? Any personal experiences that resonated?"

I blinked. "I'm not sure which research you mean," I said.

"Women criminals," he said.

Gin laughed. "What are you suggesting, Larry?" she asked. "Honey, that might hit people wrong."

"I'm sorry," he said. He seemed genuine. "I didn't mean to offend. I see what you mean." He chuckled. "Sorry, Rosa, I wasn't trying to imply—I wonder though. I had a student who became interested in criminal justice after he got arrested. It didn't quite have that effect on me."

Gin gave him a look. "What in the world did you get arrested for, Larry?"

He grimaced. "Let's just say that boys will be boys. It's not a terribly interesting story."

"No. You brought it up," Gin said. "What did you do?"

Everyone was looking at him. "Guess," he said.

I wanted to say statutory rape but didn't.

"I have no idea," Gin said.

He looked at me, apparently wanting me to guess. I shrugged.

"Statutory rape," Gretchen said. I smiled at her.

"Now I know what you really think of me, Gretchen," he said. "No. A friend and I 'borrowed' a boat from a pond not far from my house. We got charged with larceny. I can't be the only person at this table who's been arrested."

"I certainly haven't," Gin said. "If Gretchen had, I'd know about it."

Everyone looked at me. I had to come up with something.

I'd told Gin during the kidnapping that I'd never been arrested. I didn't know if she'd remember, but I also didn't want to say it exactly as I had that night. "Actually, it was for speeding," I said.

"A speeding ticket doesn't count," Larry said.

"I don't even have one of those," Gin said. "Though it's not because I haven't done it." She was embarrassed that she was such a nerd.

"I was going more than a hundred miles an hour," I added.

Everyone but me laughed.

"Were you trying to get away from someone?" he asked.

"Sort of. It wasn't my car."

"You stole a car?" Gretchen asked.

"I 'borrowed' it," I said.

They laughed.

"I was fourteen," I said.

"That wouldn't be on your record now," Larry said.

I had the sudden, unsettling feeling that Larry was familiar with my 'record.' Or Rosa's. For all I knew, Rosa might have a criminal record. She'd certainly done things that I wasn't aware of. It was conceivable that she'd been arrested. I couldn't ask her because she'd want to know why I was asking. Maybe Larry had run something on Rosa Gold and found an arrest record. If she'd been arrested, there was no telling what the charges might have been.

I finished my sandwich, wiped my mouth, and threw my napkin on the plate. I looked at Gretchen. *Let's get the hell out of here.*

"Rosa is one of the best students I've had," Gin said, trying to reduce the tension. "She doesn't realize how rare it is for me to say that. Larry, haven't you had students who awed you?"

"I have," he said. "I remember one young man in particular. He was an excellent student. Tony Spitzer. There was a slight problem. I didn't realize until after he graduated that he was studying the subject for the wrong reasons." We waited for the punch line. "He was a criminal, part of a criminal family. He'd been sent to school to get a different view, a different angle, if you will, on the criminal justice system. He eventually got caught in a big stock fraud case." Larry shook his head. "I think he's still in the pen. A brilliant guy. Just an outstanding mind."

"That sounds like something you could sell to the movies," Gretchen said.

"Funny you should mention that," he said. "I'm working on a screenplay."

I could never tell when Larry was being serious. I doubted that he was working on a screenplay, and I wasn't sure I bought the student story.

"I guess it's conceivable," Gin said, "but it sounds apocryphal."

"I think Larry has an imagination," I said. "I think you had a smart student who got involved in stock fraud. I think the part about him being in a criminal family—" I shook my head. "I think you imagined that."

Larry reached his hand across the table to shake my hand. I hesitated.

"You're good," he said. "You're right about her, Gin."

We shook hands. Things calmed down after that until dessert. Gretchen and I split a piece of German chocolate cake. Larry and Gin shared strawberry cheesecake.

Larry began pontificating again. "It's an intriguing idea, though, that someone studies something for the wrong reasons."

"Who's to say what the right reasons are?" Gin said. She'd had a couple beers. I'd never seen her drunk, but she often turned philosophical after more than one drink.

"True," he said. "I guess what I'm talking about is a sociopath. Say, a sociopath decides to study criminal justice to get an investigator's view of crime. In order to be a better criminal. Maybe a sociopath studies psychology to get—"

"A better understanding of himself," Gin said.

"No," he said. "I wasn't going to say that. In order to manipulate people better."

"If you're a sociopath," I said, "you don't need to study psychology to manipulate people. You're already a master at it. A sociopath might be better off studying something like finance or, yes, criminal justice if he—"

"Or she," Larry said.

I nodded. "If he or she wanted to use academic study for a purpose."

Everyone at the table nodded in agreement.

I toyed with the idea of killing Larry, but kept coming up with good reasons why I shouldn't. For one thing, a hit on him would alert his law enforcement buddies. What if he was investigating me? He might be the wrong person to knock off, and it might be the wrong time. Another reason was Gin. I'd already messed up one of her relationships. I didn't want to keep playing with her life. Even if Mike was a bad guy, and Larry wasn't much better, it was her life.

Something else troubled me even more. Something Rosa cautioned me about early on. She'd warned me about keeping my emotions out of killing. "You can't kill someone because they cut you off in traffic, sweetie. That's what separates you from amateurs. You're a professional. You stop being one when you become emotional."

25

A few weeks after dinner at Buster's, I was in a great mood. I'd shrugged off the discomfort I felt about the odd conversation with Larry and was feeling confident and happy. Of course, that turned out to be the day that everything fell apart.

The semester had finally ended for me. I'd turned in all papers and taken every final. I was in that state of exhilaration where I didn't feel guilty about reading for pleasure or turning on the television.

Gretchen hadn't finished up yet. She still had papers to grade and final grades to turn in.

We were sitting on the sofa in the family room. I was flipping through an *Architectural Digest*, and Gretchen was recording grades on her laptop.

"Has Gin ever slept with a student?" I asked. I was curious, but I shouldn't have asked. Gretchen was already on edge. The question set her off.

"No," she said in a sharp tone. "Gin? Absolutely not. She wouldn't do that. I'm not saying that she hasn't had crushes on students, but that's a line she won't cross. She had a couple grad assistants—She felt bad because she had inappropriate feelings for them."

Gretchen looked down at her laptop.

"What about you?" I asked.

Gretchen gave me a look. "Slept with Gin?"

She misunderstood. I was asking if she'd slept with a student. "No. I—"

"Gin's straight. No. I've never slept with her."

The room turned cold. So did Gretchen. Truth be told, she'd been chilly to me since the thing with Larry at Buster's.

"Did you ever come on to her?" I asked. I was teasing, trying to lighten the mood, but I should have kept my mouth shut. "You grew up together." I shrugged. "Like on a sleepover or something."

"No. God, no. She's not my type. She's—I don't know. No."

"What do you mean, she's not your type?" Physically, there were more similarities than differences between Gin and me.

"She's too goody-goody, I guess," she said. "I don't know how to explain it. She's like me in too many ways. A nice girl."

"I'm not." I knew what Gretchen meant. I wasn't offended.

"You've got more of an—" She waved me off. "She's like me. She likes bad boys. I like bad girls." Gretchen took a deep breath and closed her laptop. "Do you have a crush on Gin?"

I sat up straight and tossed the magazine on the coffee table. "Absolutely not."

"I'll understand if you do," she said. "It's not unusual. Students get crushes on professors."

"I don't have a crush on her."

"I won't be mad at you if you do."

Yeah, right. I doubted that very much. She was already mad.

"Look," she said "I've suspected it for a while."

Oh, for fuck's sake. Maybe that explained why Larry was so concerned about me. Maybe he thought I had a crush on Gin. There wasn't an easy way out of this. I remained quiet, thinking I'd tell her in a few minutes that I needed to go for a drive.

"You talk about her a lot," Gretchen said. "You've asked

questions. You're almost too curious about her."

I shook my head. "Gretchen, you misunderstood my question. You thought I was asking if you'd slept with Gin. I was asking if *you'd* slept with a student. I don't have a crush on her. She's my professor. I admire her. I respect her. I don't think about her like that. I would tell you if I did." I almost added, "Honest." But I'm not, so I didn't.

"I have never slept with a student of mine," Gretchen said emphatically. "And I probably shouldn't have slept with one of Gin's." She said the last sentence in a low voice.

It pissed me off, and I gave her a look.

"Actually, Larry's made comments about you having a crush on Gin," Gretchen said.

I knew it. God*damn* him. I made a face. "Believe me, that is not going on. What did he say?"

"That you seem obsessed with her."

My mouth went dry. I wouldn't be staying another semester. Larry had fucked it up.

"Why would he say that?" I asked.

She shrugged.

"He doesn't know me," I said, trying to control my temper. "Does Gin think I have a crush on her?"

Gretchen met my gaze. I threw up my hands and sighed. This was turning into a fucking disaster.

"It's not unusual for students to develop crushes on college professors," Gretchen said. She was near tears. "It happens all the time. Every semester. Students see the best possible version of us in the classroom. We're wise, well-spoken, nurturing, humorous—we've got it all going on."

"If I had a crush on her, I'd admit it." I got up from the sofa and walked around the house, gathering up my things.

Gretchen followed me to the bedroom, arms folded. "I believe you," she said, but didn't sound sincere.

"I need to think," I said. "I'm going for a drive." I felt

rotten and wanted to be alone.

"Something else," Gretchen said. She had my attention.

Gretchen waited a long time before speaking again. The air in the room felt heavy and charged. "There's something weird about your student record. The birth information is wrong. It doesn't match what you said was your birthday."

I'd made a stupid mistake. I'd told Gretchen my real birthday instead of Rosa's. Gretchen paused. "According to the record, you're thirty-seven."

I didn't say anything.

"You don't look thirty-seven," Gretchen said.

"It must be a mistake." I tried to sound calm, reasoned. "How do you know what's on my student record?"

She blushed and looked away.

"You pulled up my information. Wow. Are you allowed to do that if I'm not your student?" I asked.

Someone knocked hard at the front door. "Fuck," Gretchen said. "That's Gin."

"I didn't know she was coming over."

Gretchen left the room and went to answer the door. I was in the middle of a fucking ambush.

"I've talked to Larry. This is unbelievable." I heard Gin's loud, strained voice in the other room. "Where is she?"

I don't like confrontations. I actually glanced at a window. Before I made a move, Gin burst into the bedroom.

"You need to tell me what's going on," she said. Her eyes were flashing, and her body was in an aggressive position.

"What'd you find out?" Gretchen asked.

Gin shook from anger. "Who the fuck are you?" she asked me.

"Gin, what did he tell you?" Gretchen asked.

Gin held a yellow legal pad covered with handwriting. She glanced at it and then back at me. "Do you realize I co-wrote papers with you? If you're not who you say you are, that's academic fraud. That's my career. Who are you?"

I tried to read her legal pad. She had a lot written down.

"Her name's not Rosa?" Gretchen asked.

Gin looked at her pad. "Rosamunde Gold is thirty-seven. She lives in Miami and owns several properties. She once owned a company called Ironclad in Chicago. It was some kind of security or securities firm. I'm not sure which." She pointed at me. "The social security number belongs to Rosamunde Gold. All the tuition was paid for with credit cards in the name of Kelleher Digby. That person's social security number matches someone who was employed by Ironclad as a consultant. She lives in Stone Mountain, Georgia and is twenty-nine years old." Gin held her hands out as if to say, "What the fuck?"

"You investigated me," I said. My voice was monotone, and my face was expressionless. I have the ability to do that. Depending on what I'm doing, it can be maddening or terrifying. "Why did you investigate me?"

"Your story didn't add up," Gin said. "Did you fake any data? On the interviews? Please tell me you didn't." She took a step towards me.

"Fake data?"

"Did you make up interviews? Did you lie about findings?"

"No."

"If you did, I have to know. Everything will have to be retracted." Gin was flipping out. She wasn't this excited when I kidnapped her.

"I didn't."

"What's your real name?" Gin asked.

"Kell Digby."

Gretchen looked like she'd been kicked in the stomach. "It's *what?*"

"I'm sorry," I said to Gin. "It didn't occur to me that it would mess up your publications."

"Why didn't you use your real name?" Gin looked at her

167

pad and shook her head. "There are no criminal records for Rosamunde Gold or Kelleher Digby. No juvenile records. No credit issues. Why? Why in the world didn't you use your real name?"

She and Gretchen stared at me.

"What made you investigate me?" I was buying time.

"It was Gretchen's idea," Gin aid.

Gretchen shot her a look. "Not exactly."

"She looked you up on the system and realized you couldn't be who you said you were," Gin said. "She wanted me to ask Larry to check you out."

"Yes," Gretchen said, "and you said you wouldn't because you didn't think it was right."

They were arguing an old argument.

"Obviously," Gretchen said, "you changed your mind."

"He did it on his own," Gin said.

"Have you contacted the police?" I asked. I needed to know how much time I had.

Gin looked puzzled.

"Or has Larry?" I asked.

"He said you could probably be charged with identity fraud," Gin said, "but no one's contacted the police. I want to know why. I don't get it. You had no reason to lie."

"I can explain everything, and I will. I have documents that will explain it all. It's complicated and kind of embarrassing. That's why I didn't tell anyone."

They bought it. Their faces softened. More than anything, I guess, it was a desire to believe me. Good Lord, these people were saps. They needed to be protected from people like me.

"It's complicated," I repeated. "The documents are at my hotel. Let me go back and get them. I'll meet you back here."

I was close to getting away. "It won't take long," I said, grabbing the armful of stuff I'd already gathered.

Two Ph.D.s between them, and not one ounce of sense if

they didn't realize that I was getting out of Dodge and never coming back.

"If you're coming right back, why don't you leave your stuff?" Gretchen asked.

"When I tell you what I'm going to tell you, you probably won't want me living here," I said.

She lowered her eyes.

"I'll be back," I said. "I promise. Honest." Like most people, I lie the most when I'm trying to convince someone I'm not.

PART IV

26

I didn't rush when I got back to the hotel. I didn't lollygag either. I packed everything into my car, paid the bill, and hit the road.

I thought about leaving money behind for Gretchen. I was thinking a couple thousand in cash might be appropriate. I considered the idea a long time before abandoning it. She'd think it was insulting. That was the last thing I wanted. She might try to return it, and the drama would continue. As far as I was concerned, the whole fucking thing was over. I didn't want any contact with anyone at Oceanvue. I felt like a heel for leaving without an explanation, without saying goodbye, but had little choice.

My telephone started ringing before I left the room. Gin and Gretchen each called a couple times before I got out of California. They continued calling over the period of days it took me to drive home, and kept trying the next couple weeks before they finally stopped.

I never answered the phone, but I did listen to the messages. The first calls were reminders that I'd promised to return. The next calls were of the "I can't believe you ran out" variety. The later calls were more interesting. Gin's reminded me of the tactics I used with Thuggie. He had a bad habit of stealing ink pens, hiding under the bed, and chewing the fuck out of them. It was annoying, messy, and dangerous. If I saw him take off with a pen, I'd chase him. However, once the little fucker got under the bed, he knew how far to go so I couldn't reach him. I'd try to sweet-talk him into coming out. "Come here, sweet baby Thuggie. Mommy wants to give you kisses." If that didn't work, I'd lose my temper. "Get the fuck out of there, Thuggie, or I'm going to spank your goddamned puppy butt! Now!" Neither tactic worked. Thuggie was smart enough to stay under the bed until he chewed to his heart's content and was ready to come out.

I was like Thuggie. No matter what Gin said to me, I didn't take her bait. Her messages ranged from soft pleas to tough love sermons about how foolish I was to give up a promising academic career over a silly misunderstanding that could easily be worked out.

Gretchen's messages were painful to listen to. I preferred her angry ones where she accused me of using her, playing her for a fool, and demanding an explanation. I was used to women talking to me like that. The difficult ones were the voicemails that begged me to get in contact with her, so she could get resolution and move on with her life. She cried on some of those. I felt like a fucking jerk.

I also received emails and snail mail. I didn't answer those either. The semester finally started at Oceanvue without me. I assumed Gin and Gretchen got back to their teaching schedule and moved on. I got on with my life too. I told myself that it was a relief not to have classes. I didn't have to get up early in the morning. No more fucking homework. Yeah, yeah, yeah. I missed it, but I'd live.

I got into a routine that helped pass the time. I drove to the park every morning and walked the trails and climbed the mountain. Sometimes I spent several hours there. I thought I might run into the ghost of Hank Kingsley, and we could talk about old times, but no such luck.

I found a firing range not far from my house and occasionally stopped by to practice. I didn't think I'd go back to my former profession, but I'd always enjoyed pistol practice. It was another thing that passed the time.

I should have known that Gin and Gretchen would find it impossible to leave it alone. I'd been home about two months when I saw them on my front porch. I'd been at the park and returned to shower before going up to the firing range.

I'd gotten a late start that morning because it was Nicole's day to work on the yard. We'd spent a few minutes talking because I'd noticed an erosion problem on one side of the house, and she'd given me advice on how she could fix it.

I saw the rental car in the driveway first and then Gin and Gretchen sitting on the steps of the brick porch. I could have kept driving, but figured they'd already recognized my car. I also figured that sometimes you owe it to someone to let them scream at you. I wasn't a kid anymore. I wasn't going to run away. At least there wasn't a cop car.

I parked next to the silver Camry and got out of my car. They stared at me but didn't move. Neither was smiling.

"You found me," I said, when I reached the porch.

"That part was true," Gin said. I guess she meant my address.

"Have you been waiting long?" I asked.

"About an hour," Gretchen said. "Your landscaper said you were at the park."

I couldn't look at her. "Oh, you met Nicole," I said to Gin. "She's a gardener." It seemed an important distinction to Nicole, so I softly corrected Gretchen.

"I came to Atlanta for a conference," Gin said. "Gretch came with me. We wanted to see you. You left in a hurry. We wanted you to know we aren't angry—" She glanced at Gretchen. Always one to wear her emotions on her face, she was enraged.

Red face, nostrils flaring, the whole bit.

"What you did was really crappy," Gretchen said.

"I know. I don't disagree. I'm a liar, a fraud, and a coward." I was talking to Gin, still unable to look at Gretchen.

"I know why you did it," Gretchen said.

I finally looked at her. "You didn't deserve this. You didn't do anything wrong. I screwed up. I hurt you. I'm sorry. I'm a fuckup."

"You fell in love with Gin, and I was the next best thing," Gretchen said.

Gin squirmed and looked away.

I shook my head. "That is absolutely not it."

"Are you with your landscaper now?" Gretchen asked.

"What?" I asked.

"Nicole Westlake." Gretchen almost spit the words.

"*No.* She's been with her partner forever. She's my gardener. A friend. I'm not sleeping with Nicole."

"Did you tell her I was your sister?" Gin asked.

"What?" Where did this come from? "Why would you ask me that?"

"She said you told her your sister was a professor in California," Gin said.

Yes, I'd foolishly said something like this to Nicole, but how in the world had it come up in their conversation? I stammered for a moment and then was speechless.

"Rosa, I don't care," Gin said. "I really don't. Do you have a sister who's a professor?"

"You told me you were an only child," Gretchen said.

"What's your name anyway?" Gin asked, shaking her head.

"It's Kell," I said. "My name is Kelleher Digby."

"Why did you pretend to be someone named Rosa?" Gin asked.

"Where are the documents you wanted to show us?" Gretchen asked.

Gin looked pained. "We came here to make sure you were okay," she said. "We care about you." She glanced at Gretchen. "She's in love with you. Just tell us the truth. Whatever it is, we can handle it."

I stood there a long time, weighing things. They waited. Finally, I made my decision. Before Gin had a chance to resist, I embraced her, and said in her ear, "Have a good life."

27

I released Gin and stepped back. It took a couple seconds for her to process, but then she got it. Her face contorted. Her expression went from horror to anger in seconds. "*You*," she said. Her mouth hung open.

I willed my face to remain blank.

"What?" Gretchen asked, knowing something terrible had happened.

Gin took a step toward me. "*Why?*" She glanced at Gretchen. "She's the goddamned kidnapper. *Why?*" For a moment, I thought she might hit me.

Gretchen looked at me like I had three heads.

Gin walked a couple steps away from me and pulled out her cell phone from her purse.

"Who you calling?" I asked. "Let me guess. Larry. Before you do, let me give you the whole story."

Gin shook her head. She couldn't dial because her hand trembled so badly. She took a few more steps away from me.

"Don't call him," I said. "At least not yet. There's something I have to tell you. It'll change everything."

Gin was still struggling with her phone. I motioned for them to follow me inside. They ignored me. Gin walked further away, glaring the whole time. "No one knows where we are," she said.

"You're fucking crazy if you think we're going in there alone with you. I'm calling Larry to tell him we're at your house."

"If that makes you feel more comfortable, do it," I said. "Please don't tell him everything yet."

"Larry," she said into the phone.

I cringed. "Please," I mouthed. In a low voice, I added, "If you tell him, there's no point in me telling you the truth."

Gin gave me a look. "I'm with Gretchen at Rosa—Kelleher Digby's house in Stone Mountain." She was trying to keep her voice calm. "I'm trying to find out something. You know the address. Call me back in a half hour. If I don't answer—"

I gave her a look and mouthed "Please" again. My hands were folded in prayer.

"Just keep trying until you get me," she said. "All right. No, it's fine. I'm okay. Bye."

I touched Gretchen's shoulder. "Come inside," I said. "Please."

Dazed, she followed me. I went into the kitchen and pulled three Dr. Peppers out of the refrigerator. I handed one to Gretchen and motioned for her to sit on the couch. She did what I asked.

Gin was less compliant. She'd barely come inside the house. The door was still open, and one foot was outside on the porch. I offered her a can. She tersely shook her head and folded her arms. I motioned her to sit next to Gretchen. She shook her head again.

"Tell me what you want to tell me," she said. "I can't believe I invited you to my parents' house. With my family. What the fuck is wrong with you?"

I took a deep breath and puffed out the air. "You probably want to sit down."

"No, thanks," she said. Still holding the door open, she took a step back so that both feet were outside the door. At least she was facing me.

"I'm your sister," I said.

She made a sound that indicated she was beyond disgusted.

"I am," I said. "You're adopted. You were never told, but we had the same parents. They couldn't take care of you, so they gave you to their friends. Your parents."

"You're lying," she said. "Why would you say that?"

"Call your mother and ask her," I said. "Tell her to tell you the honest-to-God truth."

"You're sick," she said.

"Ask your mother. Gin, why would I say something like this if it weren't true?"

"Because you're fucked in the head. You've said all kinds of crap."

"Think about it. You don't look like your brothers. Or your parents. You look like me."

Doubt creased her face. It was a sad thing to see because her world would never be the same.

Gretchen looked from Gin to me and back again. Her face reddened. Her hand went to her face. "Oh my God," she said.

I'm not sure why Gin decided to do it, but for some reason she got it in her head to not only call her mom but to put her on speaker phone. Maybe her intention was to embarrass me in front of Gretchen.

"Hi, Gin," Mrs. Moorehead answered.

Gin stepped inside the door and leaned against the wall. She squeezed her eyes shut. "Mom, I'm in a situation here. I need you to be absolutely honest with me."

"Of course. What is it?"

Gin opened her eyes and stared at her phone like people used to do with radios.

"Am I adopted?" I could tell she felt foolish.

"What kind of situation?" Mrs. Moorehead asked warily.

"Mom, I'm fine. Just tell me the truth."

Mrs. Moorehead was silent for a long time. Gin looked at

Gretchen, and her face started to crumple. Like a mirror, Gretchen's did the same.

"Gin, honey, we never meant to keep it from you, but the longer time passed—then they died, and we didn't see the point—"

"So what you're saying—"

"God," Gretchen said.

"We adopted you from good friends of ours after you were born. Why do you need to know this? What situation?"

"I'm okay. I just wanted to know for sure. Did you pay for me?"

"No. For one thing, we didn't have the money. We were poor. We were students with part-time jobs."

"So you were as poor as them, but they decided they couldn't afford me." Gin was taking this personally, like my parents decided that she was too high maintenance and had to go.

Her mother was quiet for a moment. "It wasn't like that. Your father and I were on the verge of professional careers. We knew we'd be able to provide for you. They were artists. I think he made cutting boards or wooden bowls. Something like that. She might have made weavings. I can't remember. It was so long ago."

"Were they, like, carnies?" Gin asked.

"God, no. Nothing like that. They were more—I guess you'd say they were free spirits."

"How did you know them?"

"We met them at a crafts fair in Illinois. We hit it off and hung out with them." Gin's face contorted with disgust. She'd once told me that her parents sometimes joked about their foolish youth and insinuated that they experimented in their younger days. She assumed they were bragging, the way nerds do when they're trying to sound cool, but the whole adoption thing had turned her head inside out. She was probably wondering if the Mooreheads and Digbys had gotten freaky.

"No money was exchanged?" Gin asked.

She had this idea that she was sold like a wooden bowl at a crafts fair.

"Absolutely not," Mrs. Moorehead said. "We did it legally, but that was the only money that was spent. They wanted it done right. So did we. I had a lawyer friend who took care of the paperwork."

"Weren't you afraid they'd change their minds?"

"Yes. I worried quite a bit. That's one reason we moved to California. They stayed in contact, of course, and we shared some news about you. When I heard they had another child, I relaxed quite a bit. It wasn't that they didn't want you, Gin. It was that they weren't ready for you. They thought you'd have a better life with us. I never got the feeling that they were bad people. Have you been in contact with their other child?"

"You've met her," Gin said, cutting her eyes at me.

"I have?"

"I introduced her as Rosa Gold."

"Gretchen's friend."

"Yes."

"I can see it now," Mrs. Moorehead said after a moment of silence. "But when you introduced her to me with that name—"

"I know."

"What do you think of her?"

Gin lowered her eyes. "She's—different. Do Harlan and Drew know?"

Mrs. Moorehead sighed loudly. "No. I can't tell you how many times your father and I discussed this. We wanted to do the right thing. The more time passed, the more difficult it became. We never considered telling your brothers and not you. Gin, they wouldn't care. We can tell them if you want. I thought you looked like Mindy Digby. From what I remember about her."

"Really? So you think Kell and I look alike?"

"Kell. They named her Kelleher. That's what they said they

182

were going to name you if they'd kept you. It was Mindy Digby's maiden name. Now that I think about it, there's a resemblance. I can't believe I didn't notice it that day. She sought you out, didn't she?"

"Yes. Weren't they even a little upset about giving me away?"

"Yes. I don't like to think about it. She was crying. He was too. I was afraid they'd change their minds. I remember taking you and almost running out of the house. They didn't make the decision lightly." Mrs. Moorehead paused. "Did Kelleher go into your program just to have contact with you?"

"It's complicated, Mom. Let me call you later. Thanks for telling me. It doesn't change anything. I love you, Mom."

"I love you too, honey. Call me back."

"I will."

Gin wandered over to the couch and slumped onto it. Gretchen put her arm around her. No one said anything for a long time.

"At least now I know you weren't secretly in love with Gin," Gretchen finally said.

"How did you find me, and why did you kidnap me?" Gin asked.

"I was approached," I said. "Until then I didn't know you existed."

"Who approached you? Who could have possibly known about the connection between us?"

"I can't tell you. If you tell Larry, I'll deny everything. If I'm arrested, I won't say anything. How did Larry get on to me anyway?"

Gin looked at Gretchen. "I don't think he did until we said something to him. Isn't that right, Gretch?"

Gretchen glanced up at me. "He thought you were obsessed with Gin. Or maybe he thought that after we told him that your student record wasn't right." She wearily shook her head. "I can't remember anymore."

"Mike swore the pictures looked like me," Gin said. "That's why. It was you. Why did you keep conning me? Why take the classes? I don't get it."

"It wasn't a con," I said. "I wanted a connection. I didn't know how to do it. Then it occurred to me that I could take an online class with you. One thing led to another."

"What did you do before then?"

I waved off the question.

"Who were your parents?" Gin asked.

"Mindy and Gordon Digby. They were great." I teared up. "Very cool parents. Good people. They owned an art gallery in a little Illinois town. They got killed in a car accident when I was sixteen."

"Then what happened?" Gin asked.

I was trying to keep it together, so I covered my mouth. Gretchen got up, went into the kitchen, and came back with several Kleenex. She gave one to Gin and me and kept one for herself.

"How did you end up becoming a criminal?" Gin asked.

"It doesn't matter. I did things you'd find unforgiveable. I'd be ashamed to tell you. I see it as things I did. I can't and won't tell you details."

"What happened after they died?" Gin asked. "Who took care of you?"

"Some relatives for a while. That didn't work out. Then I stayed with my friend Rosa for a while. She's a straight arrow. Daughter of a surgeon. University of Chicago graduate. The whole bit. She didn't have anything to do with what happened." I needed to change the subject. "Do you want to see pictures?"

Gin didn't answer, but I dragged out a couple photo albums, sat next to her, and listlessly paged through them.

"That's them," I said, pointing at a photo of them in front of their gallery. "Mindy and Gord Digby."

It had been a long time since I'd looked at the photos. They were an attractive couple. He had long brown hair, tied back in a ponytail, and a sensitive face. She had waist-length brown hair and looked intelligent and earnest. It was hard to believe they'd been my parents. They'd been dead for almost as many years as I'd known them. I turned to childhood photos of myself.

"You looked just like Gin when she was a kid," Gretchen said, standing behind the couch, peering down at the album.

"My parents are the people who raised me," Gin said, turning away from the photo album.

I nodded. "I understand. My parents were living on campsites when you came along. They didn't feel it was right to keep you. Your parents were in a better position to care for you."

"Is that why you hate primitive bathrooms?" Gin asked. "Because your parents lived on campsites when you were little?"

I shook my head. "They had a house by the time I was born. They were settled. I was not deprived in the least." I defended my parents because Gin had an attitude about them. "We had a normal life. The house was great. Old but fixed up real good. We had two dogs. I had a super childhood."

"Were they married?" she asked.

"Yes."

"Were they when they had me?"

"I don't think so."

"Who would know more details?"

"Your parents are the best people to ask."

"You're right." Gin leaned forward. "I have to ask you— Were you sexually abused?"

"No."

"Physically abused?"

I shook my head.

"Did either parent exhibit addictive or mental health issues?"

I put up my hand. "We're not doing this. I won't be your

research subject."

"That's not what I'm doing," Gin said. "I'm trying to understand."

"Anything I did wrong is on me. Not them."

"I don't think of you as a research subject. I'm sorry. I don't understand. Tell me about the thing with Mike. How did that happen?"

"Someone wanted to con him," I said. "They knew you and I were related. At the time, I didn't."

"Who is 'they,' and how could they have known and—"

"I can't get into that. All I can tell you is that I was enlisted. Just a minute." I ran upstairs to my bedroom and returned with the yin-yang necklace. I handed it to Gin.

"I had one like this," she said, fingering it.

"Yes," I said. "My hair was cut and colored to match yours. I got glasses similar to yours. Brown contacts." I paused briefly. "You had clothing stolen from your car. I wore your clothes."

Gin looked up, stunned. "I thought I was losing my mind. I couldn't find—it was a—" She closed her eyes, trying to remember.

"A green sweater and pinstripe trousers. I was posed on a cheap motel room's bed. I looked dead. Photos were taken."

Gin scrutinized the necklace. "Mike gave me the one I wore. I threw it away afterward. I never wore it again. Yin-yang. God, he was an asshole. Did you really have a gun?"

"Yes," I said.

"You had a loaded gun?" Gin asked.

"Yes, but I know how to handle a gun."

She looked up at me. "Would you have shot me if I ran?"

I shrugged. "I don't think so."

"You don't think so." She gave me a hard look.

"I was never supposed to hurt you. That would have fucked up everything."

"But something could have gone wrong."

"There's risk in everything."

Gin shook her head, frustrated. "You registered for classes almost right after that."

"Yes. I didn't know how else to have a connection with you."

"Weren't you afraid when I asked you to come to Oceanvue that I might recognize you?" Gin asked.

"I was scared to death when I met you in your office that first time. I was afraid I'd slip up and say or do something that would make you realize."

"Then you went to the party," Gretchen said.

I turned to face her. "You think I was with you because you're Gin's best friend."

Gretchen didn't say anything.

"I was not that calculating," I said. "It was you. We clicked that night. It wouldn't have mattered where I met you. I'd seen pictures of you on Gin's phone. I was already attracted to you."

"Come on," Gretchen said. "That first night, the party at her house—" She shook her head. "You're a con artist, aren't you? What do they call it, a grifter? This house, all your money— I'm not the first or last person you've conned."

Was it better for Gretchen to think that I was a con artist or a killer? Boy, that was a toughie. "I wasn't totally honest," I said, "but I wasn't conning you. I was happy with you in Oceanvue."

"It was all a lie," Gretchen said.

"I lied about my name."

Gretchen started counting off, using her fingers. "You said you were estranged from your parents. That you were an only child. You pretended to be Jewish."

"Oh, come on. I never pretended to be Jewish."

"You left without saying goodbye. You said you had 'documents' to show us. You didn't return phone calls or emails."

"Were you paid to con Mike?" Gin asked.

I waited a long time before I answered. "Yes."

"A lot?" Gretchen asked.

I averted my eyes. "Once I found out about you, Gin, I wanted to meet you."

"You could have done it without being part of a con," Gin said.

What could I say? I rubbed my face. "I'm used to wearing masks and disguises even when I'm myself. I know it's not a life you understand."

"You went to my parents' anniversary party," Gin said. "Weren't you afraid they'd recognize you?"

"Yes, but I'd learned that once people heard the name Rosa Gold, they immediately turned me into a stereotype. Not in a bad way, but they couldn't see past it."

Gin looked at Gretchen and gave a short laugh. "That's almost exactly what you said." She turned to me. "Gretchen told me that things didn't add up with you. One of the first things she said was something like, 'Not to tap into cultural stereotypes, but does she really look like a Rosa Gold?' Remember?"

Gretchen nodded. "And *you* said it could be a married name. Or she could be adopted."

"I didn't intentionally use Rosa's name to do that," I said. "I couldn't use my real name because I was afraid you might have heard it. Or you might mention it to your parents. It was a chance I couldn't take."

"So who *is* Rosa Gold?" Gretchen asked. "An ex?"

"A good friend." I didn't sound convincing. I used to be such a good liar.

"An ex?" Gretchen asked again.

"Larry said you worked for her," Gin said. "What did you do?"

I should have known the conversation would lead to this. "I was a security consultant," I said.

They both raised their eyebrows. "What the hell is that?" Gretchen asked.

"What does it sound like?" I asked.

"You look at people's homes and businesses and then come up with a plan on how they can be safer?" Gretchen asked.

I nodded. I had to get them on another track and fast. "I wanted to meet your parents, Gin. They knew mine. I took a risk, but I'm glad I met them. I'm glad I got to hang out with you." I looked at Gretchen. "I'm glad I fell in love with you. It was a huge fucking risk. I ended up losing a lot. But if I hadn't done it—" I shook my head.

It was a con, and it wasn't. Even if true, my words were manipulative. Before a minute had passed, Gretchen and Gin were crying. And comforting me.

28

"Look," I said after they'd pulled themselves together. "Stay with me this weekend. Go back to the hotel, get your stuff, and come back. How long were you planning on staying in Atlanta?"

"Just the weekend," Gin said. "We're flying back Sunday afternoon."

"I know you've got the hotel, but you could stay here." I was mainly trying to get Gretchen to stay at the house. She was a tough nut to crack, for sure, but I figured if she stayed we'd end up in the same bed. I can put things out of my mind if I try, but with her sitting there looking fuckable it wasn't easy.

Gretchen looked at her watch. "Gin, you've got seminars this afternoon."

Gin shook her head. "Fuck it. I'm blowing off the seminars. There's no way I'm going to the damn conference."

She looked wiped out. Academic conferences can be boring as hell. That was the last place I'd want to be if I were her.

There was an uncomfortable silence. "Like I said, you're welcome to stay," I said.

They looked at each other.

"Can I talk to Gretchen alone?" Gin asked.

"No problem." I walked into the kitchen. I was sneaky though. I stood close enough to the cutout to hear most of their conversation.

"What do you want to do, Gretch?" Gin asked.

"I want to talk to her. What do you want to do? If you want to leave, I'll leave with you."

"I want to know more," Gin said.

"So do I."

"Do you feel comfortable staying?" Gin asked.

Gretchen was quiet for a long time. "I should be afraid of her, shouldn't I? I'm not. I mean, I'm afraid she's going to hurt me again, but I'm not afraid because she's a criminal. Are you?"

"Not really," Gin said. "We should be though."

They nervously giggled.

"I have to tell you," Gin said. "I know this is nuts, but there's a part of me that wonders if she's so damaged that—" She hesitated. "I've thought about getting a gun, coming back, sneaking up behind her, and—I still think it might be the best solution, but I also think it's immoral, I'd probably go to prison, and she's so damn street smart, it probably wouldn't work. It's occurred to me that if I'd had her life and she'd had mine, our situations would be reversed. I don't want to think that about myself, but I was, after all, thinking about killing her, so I must have some of whatever's in her. Don't you think?" Gin was talking fast. "I feel guilty about my good fortune. It was the luck of the draw. She could have been me. I could have been her. God, they even wanted to give me her name. I got a great life, and she got—what? A life that spiraled out of control. She doesn't seem bitter. Would I be bitter? Probably." Gin was on a rant.

"You certainly can't kill her," Gretchen said.

"I know. What am I going to do? I'm responsible for her now. I'm the older sister. Can I ever trust her? She was a violent criminal. Maybe some of it was bragging, but maybe she's killed people like she said. She held a gun on me. At the very least she's a sociopath. In fact, I don't think I could ever let her see my family again. She's dangerous."

"People change," Gretchen said. "Neither of us saw anything violent."

"That's true, but we saw a lot of the con artist. She's smart. Maybe it could be channeled in a productive way. Maybe she should be in therapy. I don't know."

"Let's spend time with her in her own surroundings. We'll have a better feel after this weekend."

"You'll be strong, right?" Gin asked. It was apparently something they'd already discussed.

"Yes. You don't have to worry about that."

I winced.

"Okay," Gin said. "We'll tell her that we'll stay." I heard shuffling. "Rosa!" Gin called out. "God, I'm never going to get used to calling her by her real name. Kell!"

I took my time coming back, so they wouldn't realize I hadn't gone far.

"We're going to the hotel to get our stuff, and then we'll come back," Gin said.

"You'll be here when we come back?" Gretchen asked with a hard look.

"I live here," I said. "I'm not going anywhere."

Gin's phone rang. She looked down and rolled her eyes. "Larry." The bastard was irritating her. She sighed. "I better take it, or he'll keep calling. I'll tell him everything's okay."

She answered the phone and strolled out the kitchen door and into the backyard.

"I'm glad you're staying," I said to Gretchen. "I know things won't be like they were." I didn't know any such thing. "I still want us to be close."

Gretchen didn't say anything, and Gin returned. "I told him that everything was fine, and I'd call him later," she said. "You've got a neat pool out there."

"You've got a pool?" Gretchen was on her feet and out the

back door. "This is really pretty out here," she said, when Gin and I joined her.

"Yeah. Nicole designed it. She's told me the names of the plants a million times, but I can't remember them."

"Is she an ex?" Gretchen asked like a detective.

"No."

Gin glanced at Gretchen. "Ready to head back to the hotel?" she asked.

After they left, I took a shower and set up the guest room for Gin. Gretchen and Gin returned a few hours later. I wasn't leaving much to chance. I wore the cut-off jeans and tank top that drove Gretchen crazy when I washed the cars.

I picked up a mushroom pizza from Stone Mountain Pizza Cafe, and we sat outside by the pool. We kept the conversation light, but there were times when the topic turned to my time in Oceanvue.

It got heavier and lighter all at the same time when I brought out a joint. I took a puff and handed it to Gin. She hesitated a nanosecond before taking it. She'd have to be out of her fucking mind to not want to get high after what she'd been through. I wasn't her student anymore, so she didn't have that barrier. I'd never seen Gin high. It was like seeing a different person. Her eyes were half-closed, and she went all Charlie Parker.

"Selective perception," Gin said. "Maybe I should do research on it. It's a textbook case. All of us were fooled by the name." She glanced at me. "How long would you have continued it?"

"I thought about doing the whole thing. Staying in the program, getting the Ph.D. Maybe teaching."

"Kell, even now," Gin said, "we could get the records changed to your real name. Yeah, it'd be a hassle, but if you want to stay in the program—"

I shook my head.

"Think about it," Gin said. "You'd do well in the field. A personality disorder is no barrier in academia."

Gretchen laughed.

Gin shook her head. "I didn't mean that the way it sounded."

"It's true though," Gretchen said.

"I'm looking to keep a low profile," I said.

Gin nodded. "What will you do?"

"I haven't decided," I said.

"Are you in contact with Rosa?" Gretchen asked. "Do you still work for her?"

"No. I talk to her occasionally, but I don't have any business dealings with her."

"Do you with anyone?" Gin asked.

I knew what she was asking. "Since the kidnapping, I haven't done anything except go to school."

That pleased both of them. Good.

"You wanted to tell me the night of the kidnapping, didn't you?" Gin asked.

"I came close."

"You should have," Gin said. "It would have been okay."

"I'm not so sure about that."

"You could have avoided the whole statistics thing with Dornan, is what I'm thinking," Gin said.

I laughed. "You said he wasn't that bad."

Gin shook her head with disgust. "Everyone says the same thing. He's a terrible teacher. Dornan sucks."

Later that night, when we were still hanging out by the pool, Gin went to use the bathroom and left Gretchen and me alone. I cleared my throat. "I've got Gin set up in the guest room. You can have my bed. I'll sleep on the couch."

Gretchen's eyes flashed. "You don't have to sleep on the

couch. I'm certainly capable of sleeping in the same bed with you without having sex."

I raised my eyebrows, but didn't say what I was thinking: Are you now?

I later showed Gin to her room and hugged her. She hugged me back hard.

"Sleep well," I said.

"You too," she said. "I'm calling Larry before I go asleep. Don't worry, though, I won't tell him what you've told me."

"I'm not worried."

"I'm inclined to give you a pass." Gin gave me a look that communicated that I was on probation.

I went back to my room.

"Is it going to bother you if I sleep naked?" I asked Gretchen.

She put her hand on her hip. "You have to wear some clothes."

"You want me to go to bed dressed?" Both of us slept nude at her house.

"At least a t-shirt and panties."

"Socks?"

"You don't have to wear socks."

Gretchen kept her back to me while she undressed. Finally, we climbed in bed. I turned out the light. We settled in. I waited a few minutes, long enough to show I'd tried, but not long enough for her to fall asleep.

I groaned and climbed out of bed. When I reached the door, she sat up. "Where are you going?" she asked.

"You're made of stronger stuff than me. I can't be that close to you and not touch you. I'm going downstairs to the couch. It's cool. Get some sleep."

"Come here." Gretchen held her arms out to me. I got back in bed, and she was putty in my hands.

Gin was making coffee in the kitchen the next morning. She shot a scornful look at Gretchen when we walked in together. Gretchen blushed.

"So this is you being strong?" Gin later taunted her. I didn't hear Gretchen's response.

We spent the day hanging out. I was relieved that I didn't have to pretend to be Rosa anymore. I was Kell, and Gin and Gretchen were getting used to the idea.

"I'll be looking for teaching positions in Atlanta," Gretchen announced to Gin at lunch that day.

We were eating at Jalisco, a Mexican restaurant not far from my house.

Gin looked at her, and then me. "I figured," she said.

"I'm moving here, even if I don't find a job," Gretchen said. "I haven't been happy at Oceanvue. I hate my dean, and I'm never getting tenure. You know all of this, Gin."

"I'm not trying to talk you out of it." Gin looked at me. "You're okay with it?"

I nodded. When Gretchen hinted that she wanted to move in with me, I didn't discourage her. Maybe I should have. I've never had a problem telling a woman that I couldn't give her what she wanted. I should have told Gretchen, "I'm not normal. Hang on to your job and stay where your friends and family are because chances are good I'll screw this up." I didn't.

Part of me wanted a normal life with one person. Of course, there was another part that was a dirty dog who wanted to fuck everything I found attractive. I kept my mouth shut and said encouraging things when Gretchen talked about moving in with me. I may even have asked her, "Do you think you could move here to Georgia and live with me?" Of course, this was a conversation during sex, and, technically, it shouldn't count, but I wasn't going to be that kind of schmuck. At least I felt guilty. Wasn't that a good sign?

29

"I fucked up, Rosa."

I'd called her after Gin and Gretchen returned to California, but before Gretchen moved in with me.

Rosa processed what I'd told her about using her name to register for classes with Gin. She was quiet while she considered how it might affect her. "What kind of grades did you get?" she finally asked. "Tell me the truth."

"All A's," I said.

"Good for you," she said. "So I've got a bachelor's degree in Psychology and almost a master's." She sounded amused.

"You're a co-author on a couple papers too," I said.

"My parents would be proud," she said.

I led Rosa to believe that I'd dropped out on my own. I also didn't tell her that I'd told Gin I was her sister. Or that Gretchen was moving in with me. Rosa could only take so much. I'd get to it.

Gretchen drove back from California with a U-Haul attached to her Subaru SUV. Of course, she brought along Bella and Thuggie.

She quickly found a good job at a nearby community college. It was a tenure track position, and she got to teach composition courses as well as some lit classes. She seemed happy enough at the new school. Even stranger, she was happy with me.

Other than Rosa, I'd never lived with a woman. I was surprised that I liked it. I've said "I love you" to women before because that's something you say when you're in bed, but I never meant it with anyone except Rosa. And now Gretchen. I did love her. I knew I did because I worried about her, mainly about what being with me might do to her. Someone, I thought, needed to protect her from me. Frankly, I was surprised that Gin hadn't put up more of a fight. She should have. I would have if she were my best friend.

I stopped going to the firing range because I didn't want to lie about it. I took Thuggie to the park every day, and Gretchen and I eased into a routine. Everything was going well, except for one little thing. Boredom.

I toyed with the idea of asking Rosa if she had anything for me. She'd told me that she was only doing the real estate thing, but Rosa was Rosa, and, frankly, I doubted it. I would have even taken a bodyguard assignment.

I talked to Gin at least once a week and emailed more frequently. I enjoyed being Gin's student, but being her sister was better. She was more open with me now, and it felt like a real sister relationship.

"Let me ask you something," Gin said, during one of our phone conversations.

"Go ahead," I said.

"Let's say a hit man did his thing. How would he be paid?" Where the fuck was this coming from?

After a long silence, she asked, "Are you there?"

"Yeah. Why are you asking me this?"

"I'm working on something with Larry."

Working on something with Larry? I didn't say anything.

"I was hoping you could give me some insights," Gin said.

"I'm not sure why you think I have inside knowledge."

"Kell, I'm not taping this. It's totally confidential. I give you my word."

"I don't trust Larry."

Gretchen snorted. "Absolutely don't trust Larry," she said from across the kitchen.

"Does he know you're calling me?" I asked.

"No," Gin said. "He won't know where the information comes from."

"Just realize the information that I'm giving you is what I've heard. I don't have inside information on anything like this."

I suspect Gin rolled her eyes. "Okay," she said.

"Sometimes it's cash. Other times, money is transferred. Or laundered through a legitimate business. It depends on who it is and how careful they are."

Gretchen gave me her full attention. She'd been mincing garlic on a cutting board. She was making sesame chicken for dinner. Only it wasn't really chicken. Thuggie carefully watched as if it were a cooking show. He was in the middle of the floor, flat on his belly, legs stretched out, his chin on top of two crossed paws. That dog was more like a cat than the cat. Bella sunned herself on the window sill, watching the birds at the feeder. It was her favorite show.

Gretchen also had a carrot cake baking in the oven. This concerned me a little. The last time someone had baked me a cake, it hadn't turned out so good.

"How much money for a hit?" Gin asked.

"Depends on who it is and how many people are involved. What are you guys up to?"

"It's for a screenplay he's writing."

"Are you writing it too?"

"No," she said. "He asked me some questions. I didn't know the answers. I told him I'd find out."

A month later, Gretchen and I flew to California for a visit.

Gretchen was between semesters and needed to finalize the sale of her house. She'd been renting it to a former student, and the tenant made a good offer.

Before we left, we dropped off Thuggie with the friendly straight couple across the street from us. Beau and Jo Jackson had two dogs of their own, and Thuggie adored them. The Jacksons agreed to feed Bella and make sure she didn't destroy the house.

Gretchen and I were invited to stay at Gin's house. We stayed in the guest room and spent most of the time swimming in Gin's pool and eating. "This is like a fucking vacation," Gretchen said more than once. I agreed.

A few days after we arrived, Larry pulled me aside. I figured he was living at Gin's, but no one had said anything, and it wasn't any of my business.

He'd shaved his big head. It made him look even more like a cop. I couldn't believe that my sister had chosen such a testosterone-laden guy, but you like what you like.

"I need you to do a favor for me," he said. "Feel free to decline."

"What do you want?" I was cool to the point of being abrupt. There were still bad feelings toward him. Gretchen, too, barely spoke to him.

"It's slightly dangerous."

I stared at him. He had a goofy look on his face like he was embarrassed about something.

"Someone owes me money," he said. "I need it picked up."

"Why can't you do it?"

"I might get shot."

I narrowed my eyes. "Why won't I get shot?"

"Because you're not me. You're a girl." He shook his head. "Look. I can send someone else. I thought—"

"I didn't say I wouldn't do it." Part of me tingled when he talked about it being dangerous. I was bored out of my fucking mind. Why not?

"I owe Gin money," Larry said. "This guy owes me money for something I did for him. It's been difficult to get him to pay. He's finally agreed to leave the money for me. Once I get it, I'm giving it to Gin."

"Why doesn't he mail it to you?"

"I have to return something to him."

Now it was getting interesting.

"What might that be?" I asked.

"A flash drive."

I licked my lips and thought. "You're afraid if you take the drive and pick up the money, he's going to hurt you."

"Probably kill me," Larry said.

I folded my arms. "But if *I* go, he has to let me take the money because if I don't come back—"

"He's fucked."

"What about your cop friends?"

"They don't know about it." He grimaced. "It's not something that I'm proud of. It's some shady shit, Kell. I don't expect you to do it for free. Name your price."

I smiled. He misunderstood. "Be reasonable, of course," he said. "You're picking up five thousand dollars."

I waved him off.

"Ten per cent is pretty generous," he said. "I'll give you $500."

"I'll do it. In return, you can take me out for dinner and explain it to me. You can keep the five hundred." I was intrigued. How did Mr. Black-and-White get into something this complicated?

"Do you have a gun?" he asked.

I didn't answer right away. I wanted to think about it. "Yes, I have a gun, but I didn't bring it with me."

"I just wanted to make sure. It's not a good idea to take one with you." Larry checked me out as though looking for a hidden gun.

"Why would I take a gun with me?" I asked.

"Don't. I'm afraid he'll think the worst about you."

"I have no intention of taking a gun. Like I said, I don't have one with me. It's back in Georgia. If all I have to do is go somewhere, pick up some money, leave a fucking flash drive—"

"That's it. Take my car. The GPS already has the address in it. Just follow the directions. It's a deserted farmhouse outside the city limits. The front door is unlocked. Take the flash drive inside the house. The money is on the floor in a box underneath the window sill. On your left, as you walk in." Larry spread his feet and pointed with his left arm. "Make the exchange. Hit HOME on the GPS and come back. It's about a twenty minute drive." He looked at his watch. "Leave in a half hour." He handed me a silver flash drive that looked like a bullet. I looked at it, wondering what in the world was on it that was so important to the mystery man.

"Another thing," he said, glancing around. "Gin thinks that you're helping me out on a school assignment. I led her to believe it's a campus-sanctioned event that involves a bit of role playing. A student exercise. I'd strongly prefer she continue to think that. Of course, you can tell Gretchen anything you want."

"I like the school angle." I certainly wasn't going to tell Gretchen the truth either. You think I'm crazy?

He nodded. "I've got to prepare for class tomorrow. I'll be working downstairs."

Larry went down to his basement office. I scrutinized the flash drive. If I had access to a computer, I'd plug the fucker in to find out what was on it, but I didn't. I'd left my laptop in Georgia. Gretchen had hers, but she was working on a syllabus. Gin's PC and laptop were in her office, but so was she.

I killed a half hour reading a draft of Gin's new book on violent female criminals. I made a few notes on a legal pad. There were things I wanted to discuss with her. I'd noticed she hadn't quoted Rosenblatt and Higgens' article about the effects of divorce. I thought it was important research and wondered if she'd inadvertently left it out. I also saw a few minor typos and made note of them.

Larry's car was a green Range Rover with all the bells and whistles. He must be doing okay in his consulting business because adjunct teaching didn't pay jack. Just like Larry said, the GPS was set up. I followed the instructions and drove outside the city. It took longer than he said, even with my heavy foot.

I found the farmhouse about thirty minutes after I'd left. The one-story white frame structure looked abandoned. The house's rusted mailbox had fallen over and rested upside down in the street. I had to drive around it to park in the gravel driveway. Most of the house's white paint had peeled off. The boards were gray and weathered. Frankly, the house didn't look sturdy. I made up my mind to go in, do the exchange, and get out without looking around, which would have been my natural inclination.

I had a funny feeling when I stepped onto the dirt patch several yards from the front door. I figured it was my nerves since I hadn't done anything like this in a long time.

The metal door knob was so wobbly that when I turned it, I feared it might break off in my hand. I swung open the door and peered inside. The interior was dark. I waited in the doorway, worried that an animal might have taken up residence. When I didn't see any movement, I looked for a light switch. Unfortunately, there was a hole in the wall where the switch should have been.

I wished I had my gun. If someone jumped me, I had nothing to defend myself with. This, I realized, wasn't the smartest thing I'd done in a while. Still, it *was* Larry. How much could go wrong?

I held the door open and tested it to make sure it wouldn't shut on its own. Then I stepped inside. The room was completely empty of furniture. I took a couple steps. Grit crunched beneath my shoes. I spied a Converse shoebox under the window sill. I went to it, kneeled, and pulled the lid from the box. It held stacks of money.

"Good deal," I said aloud.

I picked up the box, set the flash drive on the floor, planted one leg, ready to stand, and dusted off my knee.

I never heard the gun go off. Whoever was firing was using a silencer. Inches from my head, bullets shattered the window. I counted two blasts. I hit the floor and crawled away from the window. Here I was, flat on my belly, my cheek pressed to the filthy floor, scooting across rough hardwood. Goddamn fucking Larry. God*damn* him. What the fuck had he gotten me into?

I kept crawling away from the window. It was a good thing, too, because another bullet came through, showering more glass around me.

30

I briefly considered whether Gretchen was behind the ambush. She had, after all, baked me the fucking cake. It was Gretchen who'd hit the financial jackpot if I died. I'd made her beneficiary on everything. Still, Gretchen, bless her heart, was book smart but an absolute spaz about everything else. The thought of her being a criminal mastermind like Rosa almost made me giggle.

I planned to crawl until I reached the front door and then get on my feet. The biggest flaw in the plan was that if someone decided to poke his or her head through a window, I'd be easy to sight and kill. Still, I didn't have lots of options, so I kept crawling.

Until someone grabbed the meaty part of my calf. I brought up my left fist fast and hit flesh and bone. Someone groaned. It sounded male. In a second, he was on top of me, holding me down. He'd effortlessly turned me over and pinned my arms. The dude was strong. He could have snapped me like a twig.

He said something in my ear that I didn't understand. He said it again. This time I realized it was fucking Larry.

"I'm on your side," he said, loudly whispering against my ear.

"What the fuck is going on?"

"God, I think you broke my jaw. What is *wrong* with you? Listen to me. Something went wrong. We got double-crossed." He eased up his body weight. I quickly sat up. He kept hold of my arm. Our faces were close.

I felt like I was in a funhouse. How did Larry end up here so quickly, and how did he get involved in something so dangerous?

"I thought I had a deal," he said. "I got double-crossed."

"You're dealing with bad guys?" I asked Mr. Black-and-White.

"Yes."

"And you got double-crossed?"

"Yes."

"And you're surprised?"

Our whispers sounded like hissing.

"Frankly, I am," he said. "*I* was supposed to do the double-cross. I've got to get you out of here, or your sister is going to kill me."

"She told me she didn't tell you we were—"

"People lie." He let that sink in. "I figured out most of it on my own anyway. Her birth certificate was funky. I knew something was up."

"You investigated her?"

"I investigate everyone I date," he said. "You can't be too careful. By the way, I know all about you and Rosa. You've done good work. Outstanding."

I wished I could see his face better. I couldn't tell if he was being sarcastic. "How did you find out?" I asked.

"Your story didn't make sense. You weren't really trying, were you?"

"What is this?" I asked. "What did you send me into?"

"I had something taken from me a few years ago. This is my attempt to get it back. Can you still shoot a gun?"

"Yes." I didn't know if this was true. It had been years since I'd shot at a person. Larry thrust a gun in my hand. It felt like a

Glock 17. I fondled it.

"How many do you think there are?" I asked.

"Ten."

Holy fuck. I tried not to react, but I probably did.

"Joking," he said. "Two. Here's the thing. If there doesn't seem a way out, I'm giving myself up so you can get away. You came into this not knowing. That wasn't right. I never thought it'd go like this. If I start acting crazy, it's because I'm giving myself up. Do you understand?"

What a fucking gentleman. Or maybe he feared Gin more than he feared death.

"What—"

The door flung open. A figure stood in the doorway with a rifle pointed our way. I fired. The dude, dressed in a dark hoodie, dropped. Larry dumbly looked at my gun.

A second figure, this one female, suddenly stepped into the doorframe. I rolled to the side. A bullet ricocheted off the wall behind us. I fired away, and she fell.

I charged out the door, jumping over the bodies, and turned in fast circles, looking for more targets, expecting to be killed. Larry wandered out with a smile on his big face, not the least bit concerned.

"Is that it?" I asked in a hurry. "Is that all of them?"

"That's it."

I lowered my gun.

"Pretty impressive, Kell," he said.

I couldn't believe how cool he was. My heart beat wildly. I was shaking and could hear myself breathing.

Larry strolled until he was a few feet away from the two bodies. He looked to the sky, spread out his arms, and said, "Rise up, my children. You shall live again."

What the fuck?

As if in a horror movie, the victims stirred, stood, and walked zombie-like toward me. One was a young black guy, and the other was a dark-haired white girl. I fired. Nothing happened. I hurried back several feet. I must be dead, I thought. I must be fucking dead. They staggered toward me with weird smiles. They had no wounds, no blood.

The chick smiled at me and said, "Boo."

I had no more bullets. I walked backward until I fell, tripping over a broken shutter. Everyone laughed but me.

Larry reached down and pulled me up. "It was a test. You passed." He paused. "You had blanks. You've still got it, Kell. I had to make sure. Don't be mad."

I glared. "Are you fucking crazy? Those were live bullets flying around my head."

He rolled his eyes. "They both know how to shoot a gun. You weren't in any danger. Don't be a fucking baby."

"I could have been cut up by the fucking glass," I complained.

He pantomimed crying and then went deadpan. "But you weren't."

I pulled back my arm, poised to throw the gun at his head. When I finished with him, I was going to kick the asses of Dumb and Dumber.

"Wait," he said, putting up his hands. "I've got something bigger and better for you. I think you're going to enjoy it."

"You think I'll do anything for you again? You must be out of your fucking mind." I was wound up. "I don't appreciate being played. Who the fuck—"

"I had to make sure you weren't retarded. I heard you'd gone off the deep end, gotten special."

"From *who*?" He didn't answer. "*Who* is talking about me?" He didn't answer. I dropped my arm and took a step toward him. "What did you hear exactly?"

"That you went off the deep end. Just that. No one knew how or why. It's a small circle of people. You're a legend."

"You're pumping me up."

"A little. People naturally wondered where you'd gone. Imagine my surprise when I realized who you were. Here's the thing. You're the perfect piece to the puzzle I'm creating."

I glanced at his cohorts. Both looked to be in their twenties. They held their weapons in a way that led me to believe that they were professionals— and nobody's fool, despite their youth. "Who are they?" I asked.

"My colleagues. You'll be working with them. They're—"

"I don't know why you think that. Gin's not going to like this, is she? When I tell her what you did to me." I wasn't really going to tattle, but I wanted him to shake in his boots a bit.

"Come on, Kell. You know you want to." His voice was gentle and persuasive. "This is Vince and Sarah. We've been working on something for months. It'll go a lot better if we have you. It'll get done today. A one-day job. Aren't you itching to do something? You must be so fucking bored playing house with Gretchen."

We stared at each other. "Explain it to me," I said. "Don't leave out anything. There's certain things I won't do."

"I'll keep it simple—"

"But truthful. No more fucking games."

Larry nodded. "I'm giving it all to you. There's this hedge fund manager. Boy wonder. He's running a Ponzi scheme. No one's getting rich but him. Think Madoff but smaller."

Damn if I wasn't intrigued. I tried not to show it.

"His ex-wife hates him," Larry said. "She's got her money, so she doesn't care if he loses his."

This was sounding good.

"The feds aren't on to him yet, but they will be soon. A few of his clients have closed their accounts. A few more, and it'll blow apart. He's nervous."

Desperate. *Good, good, good.* I was listening hard.

"He wants a huge return on his investment," Larry said.

Who doesn't?

"He's convinced that his ex has an insurance policy that names him as beneficiary. I 'sold' it to him. Five million dollars. Not enough to cover all his bad voodoo but enough to give him time. The market's starting to improve. Maybe it'll be enough. It's got to be because it's all he has."

I had some idea where Larry was going with this. I let him continue his story.

"He's a sicko, too," Larry said. "Wants to watch—insists on seeing his ex get it. That costs extra, of course, but he's willing to pay."

Of course.

"Wants to watch a *girl* kill his wife. So here's what we do. When she's not home, we 'break' into her house. He goes upstairs and gets a good view of the driveway. The ex drives up to her house. The garage door doesn't work. She turns off the car in the driveway. She opens the car door—bam. The 'killer's' assistants grab up the body, move it to a van, and drive off. The 'killer' goes on her merry way in the victim's car."

Our eyes locked.

"A tip is phoned in so the 'body' is found, and the insurance can be paid. Or so he thinks. Meanwhile, he's given five hundred thousand to the person who made it all possible. Unfortunately, the SEC is alerted to some major funny business on the part of Rodney P. White Securities. He's questioned and knows it's over. There's no way he can say he's taken out a hit on his wife and got scammed. Wouldn't matter anyway because the insurance salesman is gone. Long gone." Larry wiped his hands.

A good con is a work of art. I didn't know a lot about Larry, but this wasn't his first time at the rodeo.

"I assume you want me to play the part of the hit man," I said.

"It's a part you can play to perfection. No one can be as convincing as you. I want you to meet with the ex first because the whole thing has to be choreographed, rehearsed, and made picture perfect."

He was right. It was perfect for me. Over in a day? Hell, that was okay. No waiting, no fucking boredom.

"I meet the ex, kill her, walk away," I said. "All in one day."

"We can have dinner with Gretchen tonight. By the way, you are *not* to kill her. Just make it look like it. That's an important point, so remember it."

I nodded. "What about the view of the driveway? Neighbors? Cars on the street?"

"Long driveway, very secluded," he said. "Unless someone's looking for it, they won't see anything."

"The weak link is the ex," I said, thinking out loud. "She's got to sell it."

"She knows that. You're the pro. Rehearse it enough times until you're sure she's got it. If we have to, we'll wait another day." He paused. "But nobody wants that. Let's get it done."

"What if it goes wrong? What if he isn't sold?"

"That's my problem It may get unpleasant. One way or another, I'm leaving with the half million."

I smiled. He had me. I wanted to kiss and punch him at the same time.

We hadn't talked money. I didn't give a fuck. I'd do something like this for free.

31

"You two ride together," Larry said to Vince and Sarah. He pointed to a white rental van that had been parked next to a dilapidated shack on the back part of the property. "Kell, you ride with me. We'll meet at the ex-wife's house. It's about an hour away."

Larry and I got in the Range Rover. "Sarah's straight," he said, before we'd driven far. "Don't be getting any ideas."

I gave him a look. "She's not my type." This was true. She had long, straight black hair that was parted in the middle. Thin and pale, she looked like a French major at a school like Oberlin. I suspected she sometimes wore a beret.

He laughed, and I realized he was just giving me a hard time. "Is Sarah your girlfriend?" I asked.

He gave me a look. "The only girlfriend I have is your sister."

"So you say."

"Do you realize that if I marry her, I'll be your brother-in-law?"

"You're *not* going to marry her."

"We've talked about it."

I slid in the seat. "God."

"Just so we're on the same page," he said, cutting his eyes

over at me, "not a word of this to Gin. Obviously."

"She doesn't know anything?"

"Nothing. She thinks I'm a consultant. Which I am. But sometimes I work in a gray area."

"How long have you been doing this, Larry?"

"Long enough to know that nothing else comes near the payout. By the way, I don't get into your area. I'm not judging. It's just not what I do."

"I haven't done it in a long time. It's not because I got religion or special or anything like that. I haven't had opportunities come my way. How many of these do you work?"

"Maybe one a year," he said. "Sometimes more. It depends on how big they are. How complicated. I was planning this one when you were Gin's student. I gave you a hard time because I got paranoid. I thought you knew something. Something didn't add up. I thought you might be police or FBI." He shook his head. "This profession brings out serious paranoia. When something doesn't seem right, what's the first thing you think?"

"The law. You thought I was going to jam you up?"

"Absolutely."

I thought about this. "Why didn't you kill me?"

Larry narrowed his eyes. "Isn't that a bit drastic?" He shook his head. "I don't do that. Like I said, I don't operate that way." He gave me a look. "Why didn't you kill me?"

"I thought about it."

"I'll bet you did."

"I'd already messed with Gin's life. I had to draw the line somewhere."

Larry nodded. "I wanted to beat myself up when I realized I hadn't noticed the resemblance. Stupid." He knocked on his head with his fist.

"When did you decide to ask me to get involved?"

"Your being here, Kell, is my doing. I convinced Gin to invite you and Gretchen. Don't say anything. Gin thinks it's her idea. Sarah was going to be the 'hit man.' But you're perfect for it. Just so there's no misunderstanding, yes, I'm using you."

I shrugged. We were on an interstate now. He turned on his blinker and took the Bloomfield Road exit. None of this stuff meant anything to me, but I was making mental notes of where we were going.

"What you and Rosa did with Gin and that jackass she was dating was a gem." He looked at me and adjusted his Ray-Bans. "Brilliant. Fucking brilliant. By the way, do you do much work with that Richard whatever dude?"

I shook my head. "Just the one time."

"Good. He's bad news, Kell." Larry gave me a meaningful look.

"He hasn't been caught, has he?" I asked, alarmed.

"Not that I know of. I'm just giving you a head's up."

"I appreciate that. How did you find out about Rosa and me?"

"The first stuff was easy. Employment, property records. Just about anyone can get that information. Afterwards, when Gin told me you were her sister, I started talking to my contacts. I learned some interesting things."

Larry took out a piece of gum, unwrapped it, and popped it in his mouth. He offered me a piece, but I shook my head. Gum gives me a fucking headache. It's also one of Gretchen's pet peeves.

"What happened between you and Rosa?"

I shook my head and glared at him.

He put up his hands. "Fair enough. I don't need to know all your business."

"Do you know people in law enforcement?" I asked.

"I know some good guys, but I know more bad guys."

"Larry, what was on that flash drive?"

"Did you look at it?"

"No."

He shot me a look like he didn't believe me.

"I wanted to, but I didn't," I said. "What was on it?"

"Binary code. It's meaningless. I was afraid you'd look at it. I hoped you'd think it meant something to someone."

I chuckled. "Pretty good."

"I gotta warn you. The ex-wife, she's not likeable. She's not only the weakest link, she's the meanest."

I figured if he bothered mentioning it, she must be really horrible. Larry drove us into a wealthy neighborhood and pulled up a long, winding driveway that led to a really cool modern house with stone, cedar, and lots of windows. Vince and Sarah were already there, waiting for us in the white van. Larry pulled in behind them.

Larry had a key to the back door and led us through a mud room and then into the kitchen. It looked like an expensive science lab. Everything was white, except the stainless steel appliances and chrome rectangular handles on the cupboards. I wanted to hate the starkness, but it actually seemed to work. Gretchen and I had talked about renovating the kitchen, so I thought I might mention it to her, say I'd seen it on TV or in a magazine.

Patty was dressed in black with gold jewelry—and lots of it. Upon meeting her, I went from "Wow, what a hottie" to "Wow, what a bitch" in less than a minute. That, my friends, is a record. Patty was so awful I felt sorry for ex-husband Rod.

"You're joking." That was the first thing she said when Larry introduced us and explained our roles. She said it in a smug, nasty tone that made me want to smack her. It got worse from there.

She asked Larry what happened to his face. I'd slugged him pretty good in the farmhouse. He pointed at me but didn't say anything. Vince and Sarah smiled.

Patty lit a cigarette, crossed her legs, and scowled at me. "I can't stand people who can't control their emotions," she said. I glared at her in a way that made her uncross her legs.

She wasn't through. Patty was a diva who wanted to write, direct, and produce the entire production.

Gin must have gotten the patience gene. I marveled at her ability to answer the stupidest questions in class without rolling her eyes or beating the snot out of some of my fellow students. I am not a patient woman. If this wasn't Larry's game, I would have gone off good on the former Mrs. White. I held my tongue, however, out of professional respect to Larry.

We held the rehearsal in her driveway, after we moved the Range Rover to the garage, brought out Patty's BMW, and moved the van down the driveway.

Larry had worked out the logistics. He'd done a fine job too. Patty was supposed to drive up and pretend to press the garage door opener on the visor. Meanwhile, she'd count to ten while continuing to 'press' the opener. When the door didn't open, she'd turn off the car and open her car door. That was my cue. I'd come up behind the car, and 'blast' her before she had a chance to get out of the driver's seat. Then Vince and Sarah would quickly pull her 'body' out of the car and take it back to the van. Meanwhile, I'd get in Patty's car and drive away. Vince and Sarah would follow me.

Princess didn't want to do it that way. She wanted a big death scene. She kept insisting that she be allowed to get out of the car, take a few steps, and then have me shoot her from behind the hedge bordering the driveway. Larry patiently explained to her several times that it wouldn't work. If it were a real hit, it'd be damn convincing and dramatic, but since it was an illusion, we couldn't take a chance on anything going wrong.

Nothing would change her mind. Larry finally agreed to try it her way. We did it five times. Each time, her death was so unconvincing that Sarah, Vince, and I rolled on the ground and kicked up our legs in amusement. Streep, she wasn't. Larry finally told her he couldn't go through with it if she wouldn't do it his way. He didn't mean it, but she didn't know that. After all that fucking wasted time, we rehearsed it the right way.

She still wasn't good. I had doubts that we'd pull it off. I also wondered if maybe I shouldn't just fucking kill her when the time came. She was a problem. Still, it was Larry's con, I was a hired hand, and I wasn't being paid to have an opinion.

It got to the point where I had to give her verbal cues: "Jerk head, slump, don't move." It didn't go well. One time, I lost my temper and tapped the gun against her head because she didn't jerk her head when I said to. She complained to Larry that I'd 'smashed her in the head.' It went on and on until I finally had to tell her that I was sorry. I apologized three times before she deemed it sincere enough.

By the time we were close to wrapping up things, Larry frowned and shook his head. "I'm worried about your verbal cues," he said to me. "What if he reads lips?"

I liked how Larry thought. He was careful and methodical, analyzing every possible thing that might go wrong.

"I don't think he's going to be looking at my lips," I said.

"That's true," he said. This seemed to reassure him.

"I could wear a stocking over my head," I said.

"No. He's paying extra to see a girl off his ex. He wants to *see* the girl."

"You could tell him I recite poetry when I do it," I said.

"That's good. He'll like that. Patty, do you know if he reads lips?"

"He doesn't read anything," she said.

After the rehearsal, I pulled Larry aside. "I don't have a lot of faith in her."

He nodded.

"Let's say she flakes—what do you want me to do?" I asked.

He looked at me a long time. "I know what you're asking. You can't kill her." He stared at me until I acknowledged his words with a nod.

"If she fucks it up, we'll skedaddle," he said. An idea occurred to him. He slapped my shoulder and went over to Patty. He engaged her in an animated conversation. Several times she glanced over at me with a look of horror. Finally, in what was her best acting performance of the day, she put her arms around him and rested her weary head on his shoulder. He looked at me and stuck out his tongue.

Finally, everyone went to their assignments. Patty left for her standard three p.m. Thursday appointment with her chiropractor. I imagined it would be a challenge today for her doctor to adjust what had to be a pretty damn tense spine. Patty was expected to return to her house somewhere between four o'clock and four-fifteen.

Larry picked up Rod, and they went to Patty's house. It had been established that Patty's bedroom offered the best view of the driveway, so after 'breaking in' the house, that's where they planned to wait.

Sarah and Vince waited in the white panel van on the street not far from Patty's driveway. The van was given a temporary sign: Benedetti Heating & Air.

I'd arrived with Sarah and Vince and sat on the ground by the hedge. I went over in my head what I needed to do. When her BMW came up the drive, I'd get into a crouching position, then listen for the engine to turn off. She'd open the car door. I'd walk to the car, reach in, and say, "Jerk head, slump, don't move." I'd step away from the car and wait for Sarah and Vince to drive up, get out, and grab Patty's 'body' from the car. I'd climb in her car and take off. Meanwhile, Sarah and Vince would throw Patty in the back, shut the door, get in the front seat, and leave the property.

We'd meet Larry at the airport. Patty would take a flight to New York. Larry would turn in the rental van at the airport. We'd leave in his car. In my head, I said the pieces over and over like a mantra.

32

Patty's car crept up the driveway. She was driving slow, maybe too slow. We'd rehearsed this too and told her that it was better to come up too fast. I clenched my teeth.

I stood and then crouched behind the hedge. I assumed Rod was watching me from the window. My movements were his cue that his ex was returning home. He probably felt a surge of excitement, or whatever you want to call it.

Patty's black car passed me and stopped. I silently counted to ten. She turned off the engine. In a moment, she opened her car door. I walked to the car, aware that I was being viewed. It was strange because in the past I'd done everything I could to avoid being seen. This freak was up there enjoying every move I made. It made me feel like a star.

I was at Patty's car door. The thought entered my mind to shoot her in the head. Am I an evil person? I thought, hmm, here's this gun, and here's her bitchy little head. Of course, it would jam up everything, and I'd be a fucking lunatic if I did, but I have to admit that there was a moment that I considered it. Do normal people have sudden, awful thoughts about harming people? Anyway, I didn't shoot the bitch.

I also didn't say the lines I was supposed to say. "Look, you stupid bitch," I said instead. "You better get it right this time, or I will fucking blow off your fucking head." Her head jerked. "Slump, bitch." She slumped and didn't move. I stepped away from the car. Vince and Sarah were where they were supposed to be. Vince pulled her out by her arms, Sarah grabbed her legs, and they carried her limp body to the van. I didn't see the rest because I slid behind the wheel, started the engine, backed up enough so I could cut the corner, and pulled out of the driveway. As far as I could tell, it had worked to perfection.

I met Sarah, Vince, and Patty in long-term parking at the airport. I got out of the BMW and joined them in the van. I tossed the keys to Patty. She gave me a dirty look. I smiled and gave her a thumb's up.

No one was particularly chatty while we waited. And waited. One time Vince asked me where I was from. When I answered, "Lesbiana," it made Sarah giggle and shut up Vince.

I started worrying. By my calculations, Larry should have shown up by now. I shared glances with Sarah and Vince. They thought the same thing.

Patty simmered. She didn't want anything to do with us. It was like we were in junior high. She was the cool kid who'd accidentally sat at the unpopular kids' lunch table.

She should have been in a better mood. After all, she'd just succeeded in pulling a big fat one over on her ex. That had to be satisfying. She was like a spoiled child who'd begged for an expensive gift, got it, and then realized it wasn't all that.

Larry's Range Rover pulled up while I was thinking about how pathetic Patty was. I heaved a large sigh. Patty looked at me. I don't think she realized the rest of us were nervous. Probably just as well. Larry got out of the vehicle with a big smile.

"You guys turn in the rental van," he said. "I need to talk to Patty for a minute, and then I'll pick you up."

Patty got out of the van, and we drove off. Vince was driving, and Sarah and I sat on the front bench.

I watched Larry through the side mirror as we pulled away.

He had his hand on Patty's arm. Grim-faced, she nodded a few times. He gave her a peck on the cheek.

"You were great," Vince said, giving me a head nod.

"You *were!*" Sarah gushed.

"Thanks," I said.

"She said you trash talked her," Sarah said excitedly, leaning into me. "She was so pissed off. What did you say?"

I winked. They laughed.

"It took you a long time," I said, after we got in Larry's car at the rental lot.

"He wanted to take some of her stuff. Loot her house. I kept telling him, 'Dude, let it go.' He went room to room. 'I'm taking that and that and that!'"

"What'd he take?" I asked.

"Jewelry, money. He took her wedding ring, engagement ring, a diamond necklace, earrings." Larry gave me a look. "I kept telling him that he was making it easy for the cops. They search his place and find that stuff? Stupid."

"Did you make him put it back?" I asked.

"I told him it was penny-ante stuff. That he was getting millions. He didn't care. He wanted it because it was hers." Larry paused. "That's American marriage in the twenty-first century."

"How'd he like us?" Vince asked.

"High praise," Larry said. "He loved every second of it. Bought it hook, line, and sinker. Kell, I think he wants to marry you. He actually asked for your number."

Sarah thought this was hilarious. "Cool," she said. "You can be the next Mrs. White. Think about it, Larry."

He did, but ultimately shook his head. "Do you know what he thought you said?" Larry asked. "He saw your lips moving. Guess what he thought you were saying."

"I have no idea, Larry," I said.

"Bye-bye, baby, bye-bye."

"Isn't that a song?" I asked.

"I think it is," Larry said.

Sara sang a few lines. Her voice wasn't bad. "It's Madonna," she said.

"Hateful song," Vince said. He shuddered. Angry women made him uneasy.

"Not Madonna. Janis Joplin," Larry said.

"Who's that?" Sarah asked.

"A singer from the last century," Larry said.

"How old are you?" I asked Larry.

"Old enough to know the difference between a singer and a lip-syncher."

"I didn't say what we'd practiced," I said while Vince and Sara tried to figure out what Larry meant.

Larry narrowed his eyes. "What'd you say?"

"I said, 'Look, you stupid bitch. You better get it right this time, or I will fucking blow off your fucking head.'"

Vince had been watching my lips. "That doesn't look like 'Bye-bye, baby, bye-bye,'" he said.

"He saw what he wanted to see," I said. "Selective perception."

"I don't suppose she reacted well to that," Larry said.

"She did it right. I said, 'Slump, bitch.' She did."

Larry shrugged. "All's well that ends well. You know what he regretted?"

"That it wasn't filmed," I said.

"*Yes*. The sicko wanted to watch it over and over again."

"*That's* marriage in the twentieth-first century," I said.

We dropped off Sarah and Vince at the mall where their cars were parked. Larry paid them both before we left. We headed back to Gin's.

I had a couple questions for Larry. "Did Patty come to you, or did you go to her?"

"She came to us."

I wondered at his use of 'us,' but that wasn't going to be one of my questions. The less I knew, the better for everyone.

"We talked her into a much better revenge." Larry paused. "I pretended to be an insurance salesman. I suggested to Rod that we could get a policy on her. It didn't take much convincing. We had an office set up on Main Street with a telephone number that was answered with the name of the insurance company."

"Did you sleep with her? You two seemed cozy."

He glanced at me. "She's not my type. Plus, I'm only sleeping with Gin."

"I know that's your official line, but—"

"It's the truth, Kell. You have a different type of relationship with Gretchen, but I don't cheat on Gin."

"What makes you think I have a different relationship?"

He made a smirky noise.

"I haven't cheated on Gretchen." I emphasized my statement with a finger stab to his shoulder. "Will you tell Gin about your—whatever?"

He shook his head. "Are you going to tell Gretchen what you did today?"

I sighed. "No. What did you tell the ex? Right before we went and did the job. I got the feeling you told her that I'd kill her if she fucked up."

"I told her that if she wasn't picture perfect, she'd end up in prison."

"You said something about me."

"I told her that people in prison were a lot worse than you. They're not, but that's what I told her."

We laughed.

"Do you ever feel like you're going to blow it with Gin?" I asked.

"If I keep her happy, I don't have anything to worry about."

"But if she finds out that you're not who you say you are—"

"None of us are who we say we are. People make up in their

heads who we are. Selective perception indeed. How much does Gretchen know?"

I shook my head and looked out the window.

He reached over and patted my thigh. "She's crazy about you. That's from Gin. She'd let you get away with murder." He smiled.

"Did you make him put back the jewelry and money and stuff?" He'd never answered my question. I'd waited till Vince and Sarah were gone before I asked again.

Larry dug into his pocket and pulled out a white handkerchief. He handed it to me. I opened it up and saw a cache of jewelry. Nice stuff.

"He gave it to me for safekeeping," he said.

I laughed. "Are you giving it back to Patty?"

"I haven't decided."

I knew then that he had no intention of giving it back to anyone.

"I'm thinking it might be an irritation fee." He smiled. "You see anything you like?"

I sorted through it. I'm not much into jewelry, but I could tell the rings, earrings, and diamond necklace were high-end, expensive pieces.

"Not my thing," I said, taking one of the dangly diamond earrings and putting it up to Larry's ear. It was pretty. Maybe not on Larry, but on the right person it'd be gorgeous.

"You see anything you want to give Gretchen?"

I shook my head and wrapped up the handkerchief. "*Way* too much explaining if I show up with something like this."

He nodded. "Don't be surprised if you see something on your sister."

"She doesn't ask questions?"

"I tell her the consulting pays for it."

"You could tell her you sold a screenplay," I said.

"She'd want to read it."

"You're right."

"Our curse—one of them, Kell—is that we're attracted to intelligent women."

"Does she think I'm a bad person?"

Larry shook his head. "She's on this nature versus nuture kick right now. She's pretty much decided that you were made into a criminal." His lips tightened. "Nature versus nurture. Nurture versus nature. I'm bored to death with it, but it's important to her."

"What do you think? Is it nature or nurture?"

He gazed over at me. "I think it's in our nature to be bad. That's everyone. Some of us like it more. Vince and Sarah each got twenty-five. Is that enough for you?"

I nodded. It was fine with me.

33

"How'd it go?" Gin asked when we returned.

"Fine," we said simultaneously.

She peered at Larry. "What happened to your face?"

"He got smart with me," I said. "Actually we had a very minor accident during the exercise. He bruises easily. Just like a little baby."

She looked at me and back at him. She decided not to pursue it.

"He's a great teacher," I said to Gin. "Wonderful with students."

She smiled. "I'm glad to hear that." She sounded genuinely pleased that Larry and I were bonding. So was I.

I later huddled with him in the living room. Separated by a kidney-shaped glass and chrome coffee table, we leaned in to each other, whispering, going over the details.

"Patty wants to spook him," he said. "Freak him out. Make him think her ghost is haunting him. Call him up and whisper over the phone. Things like that."

"It's not enough to play him for a fool, take away his money, get him sent to prison?"

"Apparently not. I've tried to talk her out of it, explain that it's not part of the plan. I can't control either one." He paused.

"She may go rogue and do it anyway. Our part is just about done. I'll make the phone call tomorrow. While he's wondering why they haven't found her body, the feds will prepare a search warrant to look at his books."

"Aren't you afraid he'll come after you? Even from jail or prison?"

"He knows me as Jack Frost. No traces."

I nodded, impressed.

"Let's face it," he said, "once he finds out that she's alive, all his revenge fantasies will be about her."

Gretchen and I left for Georgia a couple days later. Larry called me a week later with an update.

"He's been picked up," he said.

I already knew. I'd been reading about it on the Internet. The story was still small, but I expected it to get much bigger.

"He knows he's been had?" I asked.

"I think the clue bus just arrived."

"It was a good one, Larry Fine work. You impressed me, and that's not easy to do."

"I appreciate that, Kell. In my head, I'm done, but let's get hypothetical here. Let's say I get an opportunity to work something, would you be in on it?" he asked.

I felt the way an addict feels after the first syringe push. "In a heartbeat."

I looked up at Gretchen. She sensed it and gazed over at me. She was sitting at the kitchen table grading the semester's first compositions. The paper in front of her was covered in red ink. She pinched her nose shut. The essay stank.

"That's what I was hoping," he said.

Truth is, I like to do dangerous things. Larry, it seems, is the same.

I was happy when I hung up. I had a feeling he'd call again.

www.ingramcontent.com/pod-product-compliance
Lightning Source LLC
Chambersburg PA
CBHW050927120626
46552CB00001B/80